TRIALS BY FIRE

TRIALS BY FIRE

MARIE Q ROGERS

Namai Press

Other novels by Marie Q Rogers

Quest for Namai

Season of the Dove

Notebooks Hidden in an Abandoned House

Published by Namai Press

ISBN 978-1-7342413-1-0

Typesetting services by BOOKOW.COM

*For my mother
Barbara M. Rogers
who instilled in me the joy of reading
and of writing.*

Ahnti

A plant with fern-like leaves and a woody rhizome, which grows in moist tropical uplands, in wooded areas with deep soil. The plant propagates through spreading rhizomes and airborne spores. The leaves wilt and shrivel during hot, dry weather but promptly recover when they receive rain. The powdered rhizome is used in bread, where it acts as a binding and leavening agent. The leaves grow eight to ten inches tall and are edible but very bland. When wilted to the point of dryness, they have a nutty flavor and are used to flavor salad dressing, soup, and bread. If the spore heads are picked after the spores mature and before they burst into the wind, they have a sweet, spicy flavor which is used in cookies and cakes. A concoction made of the entire plant, including the spore head, has a strengthening effect for sufferers of illness, injury, old age, and grief. The flavor of the spore heads gives the tea a sweet taste.

CONTENTS

Chapter 1 Conflagration   1

Chapter 2 Awake   6

Chapter 3 Where Am I?   11

Chapter 4 New World   18

Chapter 5 No Recourse   26

Chapter 6 One Last Pleasant Evening   34

Chapter 7 Wrashiru   40

Chapter 8 Goodbye   45

Chapter 9 Motherland   50

Chapter 10 The Longest Day   54

Chapter 11 Ways of Life   63

Chapter 12 Marriage Customs   72

Chapter 13 The Weka   78

 Chapter 14 Feast of the Full Moons   87

Chapter 15 Fitting In   95

Chapter 16 Time   104

Chapter 17 Tiril   110

Chapter 18 Tale of Moses and Rila   117

Chapter 19 The Rock Fields   124

Chapter 20 Barriers   134

Chapter 21 The Light Gathering   146

Chapter 22 Eruption   153

 Chapter 23 Calamity   158

Glossary   167

Cast of Characters   168

Acknowledgements   170

CHAPTER 1
CONFLAGRATION

The jangle of shattering glass intruded into Fern's dream, followed by whomp-whomp-whomp. She bolted upright in bed, hugging the covers. Outside her windows she glimpsed, not silvery moonlight, but flickering red light. Then she smelled the smoke.

Too alarmed to be frightened, she flung aside her blankets and vaulted from bed. Safety training from school flashed into her mind. She dropped to the floor and crawled from her room, down the hallway toward her parents' room. But at the head of the stairs, the smoke was too thick. "Mama! Daddy!" she screamed. Unable to go further, she retreated to her little sisters' room. Both were asleep.

Gasping for air, Fern forced open their window, knocked out the screen, and thrust her head out. Icy coldness stung her face, but a few feet below, the roof of the back porch sloped to safety. "Wake up! Wake up!" She shook her sisters and pulled them to the window. One by one, she lifted them over the sill and lowered them onto the porch roof. They tumbled halfway down, crying in protest.

"Jump off the roof! Get away from the house. Run!" But they only scrambled back toward her.

Precious seconds ticked away. Fern yanked a couple of blankets off their beds, threw them onto the roof, and climbed out. She wrapped a blanket around each child and gave her a hug. "Run away from the house! Go get help! I've got to get Mama and Daddy." She eased each one over the edge of the roof and dropped them to the ground. By now, her little sisters had seen the fire. They stumbled away through the dappled light under the trees. Their cries receded down the driveway. She climbed back through the window.

Fern filled her lungs with air, closed her eyes, and rushed blindly to her parents' room. She opened a window and gulped air before realizing the open windows drew the smoke upstairs more rapidly. She looked down. No porch roof here, a two story drop, but no other escape.

She shut the door, grabbed her mother, and shook her. "Mama! Wake up!" Mama slumped back down. Fern groped on the other side of the bed for her father. Where was he? Her lungs strained for more air but she dared not breathe. She grabbed her mother's limp arm and managed to drag her off the bed, but how could she lift her over the window sill? As her breath burst from her, Fern shouted a desperate prayer to the heavens. Against her will, her lungs sucked in the fatal fumes. And that's all she remembered.

*　*　*

Fern felt herself falling, falling, falling. A pinpoint of light appeared, stretching to infinity. More lights burst around it and coalesced into tendrils that spun into threads and wove together to form a net. More filaments intertwined to create a soft cloud which stayed her fall. The threads of light broadened, focused, then scattered into colors like white light through a prism. Colors beyond the visual spectrum struck chords of music beyond hearing. She felt suspended outside of time and space.

A tide of elation swept over her, a sense of incredible power and strength, but at the same time, an unfathomable sadness. Was this death? The thought did not disturb her.

Fern's life flashed before her. Her earliest memories of their two bedroom bungalow in St. Augustine. Mama reading a bedtime story. Daddy pushing her on the swing in the backyard. Running down the driveway shouting, "Grandma! Grandpa! You're here!" Daddy taking her to the doctor's office where Mama worked. On the way, he pointed to the high school and said, "Fern, that's where I teach."

She came home from kindergarten one day to find Mama holding a baby. "This is your little sister." When that baby was big enough to play with, another one came. Fern helped Mama take care of them. She read them stories and kissed them goodnight. But as they grew, the babies became troublesome. Her graduation present from elementary school was a trip to the mountains with Grandma and Grandpa. She came home to find her Barbie dolls missing their clothes and some of her books wrinkled and torn. Fern cried. "I want my own room!"

"She's right," Grandma said. "She's big enough, she needs her own space."

Daddy agreed. "We can afford it now. Let's go house hunting."

One summer day, on a back road in the country, Daddy turned down a dirt lane which led through a cabbage field to a copse of live oak trees. There, hidden by weeds and five foot tall azalea bushes, stood a weathered, two-story farm house.

"Whatever are you doing?" Mama asked, but Daddy jumped from the car, made his way through the undergrowth, and climbed the porch steps. When he opened the door and went inside, Mama sighed. "You girls stay here." But the little ones cried for their mother and resisted Fern's efforts to distract them. She had no choice but to take them to the house.

Their parents stood in the empty living room.

"This isn't what I had in mind," Mama said.

With his pocket knife, Daddy scratched some peeling paint from a door post, exposing the wood. "This house must be a hundred years old. It's made from heart of pine. Termite proof."

"You mean fat pine. Lighter wood. It's a firetrap."

"It's perfect! We can do most of the work ourselves and we'll end up with more house than we could ever afford to buy."

"But it's not for sale."

They bought it anyway. Fern enjoyed helping with the renovation, but it seemed to take forever. The family spent weekends camping on the property to work on the house. Fern's parents took extra jobs so they could afford to hire craftsmen for work they couldn't do. She turned twelve before they moved in.

That year was the happiest of her life. At last, she had her own room. Her father set up a telescope in the backyard and on clear nights the family would view the stars. Fern had previously dreamed of becoming an astronaut. Now she wanted to be an astronomer.

One evening, they went to the beach to watch a nighttime launch of the space shuttle. As the ship rose to the heavens in a blaze of magnificence, Daddy gripped Fern's shoulders and said, "There is the future! Your children and grandchildren will populate the stars." Her sisters giggled, but a cloud of foreboding shuddered through Fern.

That ominous feeling returned on her thirteenth birthday when they went to Disney World. The park was crowded and lines were long. Fern amused herself by observing other people. Waiting in line for Small World, she noticed a family with dark, not quite black, hair and olive skin. The daughter's hair hung to her waist like a veil. She turned and met Fern's gaze. Her eyes were not brown, but green, a deep green like that of the sea. Fern perceived no hostility, only curiosity, but those eyes engulfed hers, as if the girl could see into her very soul. Despite the heat of the day, Fern shivered.

The line moved. The girl's family turned a corner and Fern lost sight of them. Her delight in Small World had been spoiled. The cute music irritated her. The dancing dolls from around the world seemed sinister. For the rest of the day, she scanned the crowds looking for that girl, but she seemed to have disappeared.

After this, for no reason she could determine, the stars frightened Fern. No longer did she want to be an astronomer. Too embarrassed to tell her parents about her fear, she resisted joining the family for stargazing. If her father insisted she look through the telescope, she closed her eyes. She was grateful for the magnolia tree that shaded one of her windows and the live oak that screened the other. At least she had a sanctuary where the stars didn't intrude.

On Christmas Eve, they roasted pecans in the fireplace. Suddenly, a log split with a loud pop and a burning ember flew out, nearly hitting Fern, and landed on the carpet. Daddy ran for water. Mama grabbed the ash shovel and scooped up the ember. Then she set the screen across the hearth and said, "We don't need a repeat of this."

A few weeks later, an ice storm knocked down power lines, so they used the fireplace for heat. Fern woke that night to a frosty stillness. She got up to put on socks and heard movement downstairs. Her father was building up the fire. Fern went down to warm herself.

"What's wrong?" Daddy asked.

"Just cold."

"It'll be warm in a few minutes. Heat rises, you know."

Fern nodded and stood with her back to the fire. Soon her back felt toasty, but her front was still cold. For several minutes, she stood in front of the fireplace, turning to warm one side, then the other, until she got sleepy and told him goodnight.

"Goodnight." He kissed her on the forehead. She hugged him.

As she climbed the stairs, Fern glanced back. This picture was forever imprinted on her mind—her father relaxing in his chair by the hearth, sipping a beer. The screen sat beside the fireplace, the blaze lighting the room. Fern had a vague, uneasy feeling.

She groped through the shadows to her room, leaving the door open for warmth. She closed her eyes against the brilliant moonlight and the icy silence outdoors and fell asleep.

Until the jangle of shattering glass woke her.

* * *

Suspended between worlds, Fern stretched out a strand of consciousness. It met something familiar and secure which cradled her, gently lowering her to the ground.

It was dark but she could breathe now, fresh warm air. Her bare skin rested against cool, wet grass. Instinctively, she reached out and murmured, "Mama?"

"Fern," came her mother's voice, then her hands, her arms. Safe at last, Fern drifted back to sleep.

CHAPTER 2
AWAKE

Fern woke in a hospital room. Her mother lay across the room on the other bed, with a breathing mask over her face. Fern touched her own face. She didn't have one. An herbal scent wafted through the air. She took a deep breath. No trace of smoke in her lungs. She extended her fingers and toes. Her body seemed intact but too heavy to move. She tried to recall how they got out of the fire, but her last memory was of dragging her mother out of bed. How had they managed to escape? She inhaled the scented air and settled back into slumber.

She dreamed of her father. They were in the back yard, exploring the cosmos. His voice was only a faint murmur, but her vision followed his arm beyond the finger that pointed to Saturn. She put her eye to the telescope and could see forever, to the limits of the universe.

Fern half-woke. At one time she'd enjoyed those astronomy lessons. What happened to her father? She opened her eyes and looked at Mama's bed. It was empty! She jerked her head up from the pillow and raised up on one elbow. Her mother sat in a rocking chair nearby. Fern tried to sit up but fell back, exhausted. "Mama, what happened?"

Mama's eyes sagged and the skin around them looked bluish. "I'm not sure." Her voice was labored. "The house burned down."

Fern's heart ached to the pit of her being. She began to cry. Mama moved to her bedside and put her arms around her.

"Is everything gone?"

"Yes. Everything. Everyone." She laid her head against Fern's. "You saved my life. I don't understand how."

The door opened. A nurse glided into the room and set two cups on the bedside table. Fern's mother struggled to stand. The nurse helped her back to the chair. Then the woman turned to Fern and said, "Hello, my name is Lila."

Fern said, "I'm Fern." Then she felt foolish. Of course the nurse would know her name.

Lila smiled, laid a hand on Fern's forehead, and took her wrist with the other. She smiled again and nodded. "You will be fine. Can you sit up?"

With Lila's help, she did. Lila supported Fern's back and handed her a cup of tea. Fern drew in the delicate aroma, similar to her father's chamomile tea, and began to sip. The tea could use some honey, but she didn't complain. Its warmth spread through her body, and with it the comfort of an unseen embrace.

Lila's attention turned to Fern's mother, "How do you feel?"

"About the same, I'm afraid. I still can't sleep." She took the other cup from Lila and sighed. "What I wouldn't give for a cup of coffee."

"We could concoct a suitable substitute, if you could tolerate it. Meanwhile, let's see if you can drink this."

Fern's mother took one sip, hastily set the cup down, and gestured desperately. Lila handed her a basin and she vomited. Fern peered into her own cup and put it down. Lila produced a moist towel and a bowl of water so Fern's mother could rinse out her mouth. "I'm sorry. I'll try later." She looked at Fern. "Drink yours. It's good for you."

Fern was thirsty and eagerly finished her tea. Then, feeling sleepy, she lay down.

She dreamed about her father again, this time of their trip to the beach to watch the space shuttle. The dream was so real, she woke with the impression that she still stood on the beach watching the contrails disperse.

Afternoon sun slanted through the window. Fern sat up, feeling stronger. Mama sat in the rocking chair, shoulders slumped, wincing with each breath. Her mouth smiled at Fern but her eyes drooped.

"Mama, what hospital are we in?"

Mama narrowed her eyes. "What do you mean?"

Before Fern could respond, another nurse came in with more tea. In an accent Fern couldn't place, she said, "Hello, I am Andli." She checked Fern's forehead and pulse, smiled, and quietly withdrew.

Fern drank the tea. "You didn't tell me where we are."

"I'm not sure."

"Are the little girls here, too?"

Mama began to sob, then went into a choking fit. Andli returned with something Fern perceived as a breathing machine. She handed her patient a mask to cover her mouth and nose. When Andli turned on the machine, a fragrant mist dispersed into the air. Fern's mother inhaled the vapor, her skin glowed pink, and she breathed more smoothly. After a few minutes, she squared her shoulders. With Andli's help, she moved to Fern's side, put her arms around her, and whispered, "I'm afraid our babies perished in the fire."

Fern nearly leaped from her arms. "No! I put them out the window, on the ground. I told them to go get help."

"Did you? Really? Are you sure? Did they go for help?"

"I think so. They were going down the driveway."

"And your father?"

Fern looked down and shook her head. "I couldn't find him." Mama's arms tightened around her.

"The girls might be with Grandma and Grandpa."

Her mother's apparent confusion puzzled Fern, but a familiar sensation diverted her thoughts. She whispered, "I have to use the bathroom." She tried to stand, but her legs wobbled.

"Don't get up." Supporting herself with the bedside table, Mama returned to her chair. "Let Andli help you."

Despite embarrassment, Fern let Andli help her with a bedpan. Afterward, Andli left with the bedpan and returned with another cup of tea. Fern suspected the tea held a sedative. It made her sleepy again.

Now she dreamed about her birthday, riding the boat through Small World. One of the dolls, with long dark hair and green eyes, looked directly at Fern and said, "Your children and grandchildren will populate the stars."

Fern cried, "No!" and ran all the way home, upstairs to her room, jumped into bed, and pulled the covers over her head.

"Fern! Are you okay?"

She woke in the hospital room, struggling with her blanket. Mama perched at the edge of the rocking chair. Fern shook her head to clear it. "Yeah. I'm all right. Just a bad dream."

A tall doctor with a beard came in. "Hello, I'm Taran," he said in a rich baritone voice.

Fern couldn't help staring at his hair. It was braided in tight cornrows, similar to a black person's, but while Dr. Taran was dark skinned, he was not black. His beard was also plaited, in a manner like a Viking's. Yet when he took Fern's hand, she felt immediate trust. She looked up into his eyes. Where had she seen eyes like these? A deep, soft green, like that of the sea?

"You seem to be mending well," he said.

"Yes, sir. When can I go home?" She shook her head and blinked away tears. "I mean, get out of here?"

"When you are as well as we can make you." He gestured about the room. "Tell me what you see."

What did he mean?

"Describe this room."

Was this was a test of her wellness? "The walls are green, the floor is brown. There are two beds, a rocking chair, this table, a breathing machine." She looked around again. Although Fern had little experience with hospital rooms, some things—she couldn't say what—seemed to be missing. "No flowers."

"What do you see out the window?"

"Palm trees, pine trees, some others—I don't know what kind." Why didn't she know? Her father had taught her all about trees. She looked beyond them to the sky. "It looks like it's going to rain."

He smiled. "You'll be fine. You just need to stay with your mother until she's ready to leave."

"What about the hospital bill?"

He laughed. "You don't need to worry about that." He turned to her mother and in a low voice said, "Don't worry about your daughter. She has found her own way to deal with shock. Give her time to heal. Have you been able to sleep?"

"No. Not at all."

"Would you like to try again to drink something?"

"It's no use. I can't even tolerate water."

"You know we've done all we can."

"I know. And I'm grateful." She sighed deeply, then coughed. "Just take care of my Fern for me."

"You know we will."

Fern only half-listened to this exchange, but the mention of drinking reminded her of the tea that filled her bladder. "Is it okay if I get out of bed?"

"Certainly," Dr. Taran said. "Just take it slowly at first."

Fern swung her legs over the edge of the bed. She adjusted her hospital gown and stood up slowly to let the unsteadiness dissipate. "I need to use the bathroom."

But she'd taken only a few steps toward the bathroom door when someone else entered the room.

Fern found herself drowning in deep, green eyes—face to face with that strange girl from Disney World! The girl now wore a green tunic, and her hair was elaborately plaited, but without doubt, it was she.

The hospital room fell away. Fern's gown turned into a loose tunic, the beds to wooden cots, the breathing machine to a bowl of steaming stones, the walls and ceiling to the interior of a thatched hut with reed mats on the floor. The "doctor" wore a tunic, not scrubs. The only things that didn't change were the people themselves and the rocking chair.

It dawned on Fern—outside it was summer. The last she knew it had been winter. A thunderclap sounded. Fern's bladder emptied.

Mortification kept her from fainting, but her legs collapsed. From a sitting position on the floor, she looked up at her mother. "Where am I?"

CHAPTER 3
WHERE AM I?

Dr. Taran answered, "Let's get you comfortable, then we'll explain."

Fern looked at him closely. He was the man she'd seen at Disney World. Dazed, she let the girl help her to her feet and lead her outside where Andli met them. Fern's eyes followed the girl back to the thatched hut. How could she have mistaken it for a hospital?

A wooded area surrounded her. She glanced at the unfamiliar vegetation, but her mind could not absorb it all. Andli took her hand. Fern focused on her. She, too, had green eyes and dark hair, braided and coifed much like Dr. Taran and the girl. She was a small woman, not much taller than Fern. No, Fern had not seen her at Disney World. She took comfort in that. Like Taran, Andli emanated trust. She led Fern down a green slope to a stream and indicated that she should enter the water. Its warmth soothed her. Andli apparently didn't speak English but made motions that Fern should take off her tunic. She sank into the water and did so.

Andli reached for the tunic, took it downstream, rinsed it out, and laid it over a large black rock. She returned to Fern and plucked a leaf from a plant on the bank. Fern watched her crush the leaf and rub it in her hands, working up a lather. Then she handed it to Fern with a nod. Fern began to wash herself.

Thunder rumbled in the distance. Andi looked at the sky, held up her index finger, and left. Naked and alone in this strange place, anxiety threatened to morph into panic. A breath of wind touched Fern's face, as soothing as the water. Her muscles relaxed. She looked around. Trees nodded in the breeze. Shrubs bent over the stream. It was beautiful.

By the time Fern finished bathing, Andli returned with a fresh tunic and a large cloth which she held up, hiding her eyes behind it. Fern assumed it was a towel. She glanced around to be sure they were alone and stepped out of the water into the towel. After she dried off, she wriggled into the clean tunic.

Thunder again. Dark clouds loomed above the trees. The wind blew a rift in the clouds, revealing a mountain. Fern stared. Was she seeing things again? Andli took her hand and led her back to the hut.

That girl was sitting on Fern's cot. Fern glared at her.

"Sorry," the girl said, stood up, and left.

The urine soaked mat had been replaced by a fresh one. Dr. Taran sat on the other cot and Andli joined him. Fern took her seat and looked at the adults. "Well? Where on Earth are we?"

Mama giggled almost hysterically, coughed a little, cleared her throat, and took a breath. "We're not. I…" She shook her head. "I don't know how to say this except, it seems that we are on another planet."

"Huh?"

Dr. Taran nodded. "It's true."

"What?"

All three adults nodded.

Fern looked at each one. "Are you serious?" They were. "But—but how?"

Her mother's voice was a scratchy whisper. "No one understands how you did it, Fern, but somehow you brought me—you brought both of us here."

Fern grimaced and shook her head. No. Impossible! Mama wouldn't say anything so preposterous. Was she still hallucinating? Had they died in the fire after all?

"No, we're not dead," Mama said. "I know it sounds impossible. I have trouble believing it…" Her voice gave out.

Dr. Taran spoke. "You were both trapped in the fire and had no way to escape. Apparently you weren't ready to die, so you found another way out. You transported yourself and your mother here."

"I what?"

"We call it 'wrashiru.' You transcended the usual boundaries of space/time to come here. And you brought your mother."

Fern shook her head rapidly. "No. No."

"Look around you, Fern. What do you see? You can trust your eyes now."

Yes, she sat inside a primitive thatched hut, but such places existed on Earth. Dr. Taran and Andli were barefoot and dressed in colorful tunics. Both looked human enough, although they didn't resemble any native people familiar to Fern. Taran's appearance had changed since she'd seen him in Florida. At Disney World, he'd looked like any other tourist. The man before her was decidedly exotic. Somehow, she'd been transported from a Florida winter to someplace warm, with mountains and unfamiliar vegetation. But another planet? "That's only science fiction. It can't be done."

"But it can be, and it is done," Dr. Taran said. "Some of us can do it. You saw me and Lila and Tira at Disney World. How do you think we got there?" He grinned. "Have you seen any UFOs lately? We were returning here at the same time you were caught in the fire. You seem to have hitched a ride with us. That's probably why you ended up here and not somewhere else on Earth. I'll explain more later, when you're ready. What amazes us is that you were able to do it with no training. What we find miraculous is that you brought another person with you. We've never known that to happen before."

Fern tried to absorb this. She shook her head again. "But why did this look like a hospital room a little while ago?"

"Self-hypnosis. Your mind tried to cushion you from a shocking revelation." He leaned forward. "You were unconscious when we found you. Your mother wasn't. We told her we were taking both of you to a healing place. Your mind probably translated that to 'hospital,' so when you woke up, you saw what you expected." He paused. "By the way, I'm not a doctor. Andli is the healer."

Andli smiled at Fern. Her eyes were a darker color than Taran's or Tira's. As Andli's eyes gently held hers, Fern's brain began to untangle. She broke the gaze and looked at Mama, who said, "What he's telling you is the truth."

In a small voice, Fern asked, "So, how do we get back home?"

Andli gave her a sad smile. Taran and her mother exchanged glances. Finally, Mama lowered her eyes and said, "We don't."

Fern's body turned to stone. Her eyes lost focus. A roar of silence filled her ears. Her lungs did not ask for air. Deep inside, Fern became aware of a choice—breathe or die. Although it hurt, she drew a deep breath.

No one said a word. Fern whispered, "Why not?"

Taran's voice was soft. "We tried sending you back. We tried using a guide to take you. We were not successful."

Outside, the wind rose and a few raindrops splattered on the roof. All three adults looked upward as though they could read the weather through the thatch. Taran said, "Andli and I need to go home before it storms. We'll talk more later. You need to rest. Don't worry about the storm. You'll be safe and dry as long as you remain here." They left.

Fern couldn't rest. "Do you really believe that nonsense, Mama? What if they kidnapped us? Do you have any idea where we really are? They *made* me see a hospital room. They're trying to cover something up." Lightning flashed in the darkening sky. The hut seemed to shake with the thunder.

Mama couldn't speak above a whisper. "Fern, why would anybody kidnap us?" She coughed. "If anyone had told me this stuff before, I wouldn't have believed them. You were lucky, you lost consciousness when we got here. I didn't. I seriously thought I'd lost my mind." She paused to catch her breath.

"Fern, there are some things about you. There've been times that, if I'd believed in such nonsense, I'd have thought you had ESP. You seemed to know things you had no way of knowing. Or you'd say something was going to happen, and it did. I'd chalk it up to coincidence. At times, you'd say something I was thinking. I just thought we were thinking along the same lines. Now I'm not so sure. Now I think you may have abilities I never dreamed of." She moistened her mouth with a damp cloth. "I do know you took us out of that burning house. You saved both of our lives. I believe Taran."

The wind blew through the open window. Rain thrashed outside. Fern had no recollection of those things her mother said she'd done. "Well, if all this is true, I wish we hadn't come here." She got up to close the window but found no screen, pane, or shutter. To her surprise, none were necessary. The rain didn't blow in.

Mama's lips moved. Fern had to lean in close to hear her. "We can't change that now. Unless you can take us back in time. Fern, please sit down and tell me what happened that night."

While the storm spent its rage, they sat on Fern's cot and she related all she remembered. When she told about putting her little sisters on the ground and sending them for help, she felt a drop of moisture on her arm. She looked up to see if the roof leaked, but the thatch remained dry.

Her mother hugged her tightly. Another tear fell. "Bless you, Fern. I thought they were dead, that only you and I survived. Now I'm sure they're safe. They must be with Grandma and Grandpa." She tried to clear her throat. "But you couldn't find Daddy?"

Fern sobbed. "Not in your bed. I didn't have time to look anywhere else."

"Of course you didn't. You'd already done more than could be expected. If he was still…" She choked. "Downstairs…."

Fern cried in her mother's arms. "But if I have ESP, why didn't I know it would happen? I could have stopped it!" That uneasy feeling she'd had when she went back to bed that night—the image of her father at the fireside —flashed through her mind. Had that been a warning? Why hadn't she heeded it?

"Don't…ever…blame yourself for what happened." She smoothed Fern's hair. "From what I've heard about ESP, it's not very reliable. Maybe that's why scientists can't prove it."

The storm abated. Fern looked around the hut. Not a drop of rain had entered.

"Fern, when you were downstairs that night, was the grate across the front of the fireplace?"

"No. Daddy was putting wood on." That last glance at him again, relaxing in front of the open hearth. Her heart was an empty well.

Mama looked out the window. "I didn't even know he'd gotten out of bed." She sighed and returned to her cot. "I need to lie down."

When Fern lay back on her bed, she heard a rustling sound, accompanied by an almost minty aroma. Mama said, "The mattresses are stuffed with fragrant leaves."

After the rain stopped, before night fell, Taran and another woman brought Fern more tea, a bowl of vegetable soup, and some biscuits that tasted slightly like peanut butter. Andli brought another bowl of hot rocks and an infusion which she poured over them, releasing a sweet, aromatic steam. Fern's mother inhaled, then smiled and whispered, "Thank you. The imbwina always helps me breathe easier." Andli smiled.

Taran looked at Fern. "Is there anything else you want to ask me now?"

Fern tried to think. She shook her head. The only thing she wanted was to go home.

"You know we're available if you need us. Just call out the door, and someone will come. I hope you rest well."

After they left, Fern examined her vegetables but couldn't identify any of them. She found the food satisfying, but the tea made her sleepy again. First, though, she had other needs. "Mama, where's the bathroom?"

"There's a latrine, I don't know where. I haven't been able to go." She waved a hand. "Just go outside somewhere."

"You know, they didn't give me any panties."

"I know. I don't think they wear them here."

Fern went around to the back of the hut where no one was likely to walk. A moon high in the sky lighted her way. The still-wet grass caressed the soles of her feet. No, it was not grass but a low-growing ground cover. With no toilet paper, she used leaves. She washed her hands in the stream and thought about brushing her teeth. On a whim, she broke off a leaf of the soap plant. The taste was not unpleasant, so she cleaned her teeth with it, using her fingers. As she returned to the hut, another moon peeked through the trees. She glanced up at the one overhead and rushed inside. "Mama! I just saw…"

"I know. Two moons."

CHAPTER 4
NEW WORLD

Fern tried to sleep. She had nothing to read. The hut had no lighting, anyway, not even a candle. Every time she turned over, the mattress rustled annoyingly, but her movement released its bouquet. Finally, she lay still and let the scent quiet her. Music and singing in the distance lulled her to sleep.

She woke during the night with the need to relieve herself again. Her mother appeared to be dozing in her chair. When Fern tiptoed by, Mama said, "You don't have to be so quiet. I'm awake." Outside, Fern gazed in awe at the two moons. Then she glanced at the dark forest and shivered. What might prowl there at night? Her fear was quelled by a benign presence that issued from the trees. Back inside the hut, she felt safe, even with no door.

Later, a clamor woke her.

Mama beat her fists on the arm of the chair. "You stupid fool! You goddamned stupid fool! Why didn't you listen to me? Why weren't you more careful? I told you what could happen. Now our babies have no home, no mother, no father…" Her voice deteriorated to a hacking grunt.

Fern jumped out of bed. "Mama!"

"I'm sorry."

Fern crouched beside the chair and put her arms around her mother.

"I'm sorry. I'm just so mad at your father. I—never mind. Fern, I'm sorry. You shouldn't have to listen to this. I'm sorry I woke you."

"Daddy didn't mean for it to happen. It was an accident."

"I know. I really love your father. I'm just…."

"I know. It hurts." She laid her head on Mama's lap.

* * *

Would the night never end? Finally, a gray light stole into the hut. Fern relaxed in the promise of morning's approach. She heard a brief song in the distance, and shortly afterward, Andli and Taran returned with fresh imbwina—the bowl of hot stones and herbal inhalant. Fern's mother readily breathed in the vapor. Then Taran asked her, "How are you feeling?"

"I am at peace."

A woman and man arrived with food. Taran introduced them as Rina and Doran. Like the other people she'd met, this couple wore tunics and no shoes. Both were well tanned, with green eyes and plaited hair. Fern looked at her breakfast—vegetable soup, biscuit, and tea—the same as supper. Is this all they ate here? Was there a medical reason for this diet? Were these people vegetarians? But the food was tasty, so not wanting to seem ungrateful, she didn't ask.

Andli left with Doran, but Rina stayed and began to comb Fern's mother's hair, stroking the locks until they fell in golden waves. Fern put a hand on her own head. She hadn't even thought about her appearance. How did her mother manage to look nice despite illness and lack of cosmetics? After Fern finished eating, Taran said, "Rina will comb your hair, if you like."

Fern nodded and Rina set to work on Fern's snarls. But she didn't pull, only massaged the unruly strands with finger and comb. Mama smiled. "Fern, you may find yourself the center of attention here. Most of these people have never seen blonde hair or blue eyes. The children kept wanting to play with my hair."

When Rina finished, she handed the comb to Fern. It was made of reddish wood and the shape of the handle nestled into her palm as though it had been carved to fit. Fern ran her fingers along the grain of the wood. Silky smooth, it caressed her fingertips. "It's beautiful." She handed it back to Rina, who said something in a strange language and, with a gesture and a smile, indicated it was a gift. "Thank you," Fern said.

Before he and Rina left, Taran said, "Fern, you would do well to walk about today. My daughter Tira will come and show you around. She's the only other person here right now who speaks English."

Fern didn't relish hanging out with Tira. "Mama, I really should stay here with you."

"No, Fern. I'll be fine. I'm sure you're tired of being cooped up."

Yes, and she was curious to see this new world. "What about that other lady, the nurse. She spoke English."

"Lila? She may have gone back to her family. They live near the ocean."

"I thought she was Taran's wife, Tira's mother."

"No, they're cousins. Andli is Tira's mother."

Fern thought back to Disney World. She didn't know those people then, but she'd had a distinct impression that the man and woman were a couple. "How do you know all this?"

"Don't forget, I've been awake since we got here. I had a lot of opportunity to talk to them. Lila's been away from her family for a long time and wanted to go home."

"How long was I unconscious?"

"Three days."

Three days! She recalled dreams that had occurred after she first woke, but nothing from those three days.

"I really worried about you, but they assured me you were going to be all right. They said that when they do the wrashiru, they need time to recuperate, and since you were totally untrained, you needed more time. They said that your being unconscious gave your body and brain the time it needed to heal properly."

Tira arrived, wearing a wide-brimmed straw hat woven with designs of colorful thread. She handed Fern a similar hat, not quite as fancy. "You'll need this, especially since your complexion is so fair. And your eyes will be sensitive to our sun's rays."

"I know," Fern huffed. "I've lived in Florida all my life."

"Fern," her mother said, "you need to take more precautions here than we did at home. The UV rays are more intense."

Fern acquiesced.

Without her having to ask, Tira took Fern to the latrine. This was a narrow ditch in the woods, one end covered with fresh soil. A small wooden spade poked out of a nearby pile of dirt. Tira pointed to a basket of fuzzy leaves. "That's what we use for toilet paper." She straddled the ditch to demonstrate how to use it. Fern averted her eyes and silently questioned the level of civilization here. After Tira finished, she shoveled dirt over her business.

Fern sniffed. She detected no objectionable odor. "Is this the women's latrine?"

"No, everyone uses the same one." Then, as though she sensed Fern's unvoiced concern, Tira turned her back to let Fern use the latrine in privacy.

They walked along a path through the woods. Fern now paid more attention to her surroundings. The forest floor was soft under her feet. The air had an earthy smell. She marveled at the size of the trees, not only their height but their girth, two or three times as wide as the old live oaks that had surrounded her house. Some resembled pines but there were also broadleaf trees. She debated whether the smaller trees looked more like palms or ferns. The sparse underbrush was mostly low shrubs with wide leaves, lianas climbing into the trees, and smaller vines that clung to other vegetation. She asked Tira the names of the trees but was too overwhelmed to commit them to memory. She recalled her concern from last night. "Is it safe in these woods?"

Tira acted surprised. "Of course. Nothing here will harm you, unless you fall out of a tree or something."

"What about wild animals?"

Tira laughed. "None here."

A leaf brushed Fern's arm and she swatted at it.

"What's wrong?" Tira asked.

"I thought it was a mosquito."

"We don't have mosquitoes here, either."

"Really? That's awesome. Is there anything that bites?"

"No. There's no animal life on this world."

Fern knit her brows and pondered what she knew about evolution and ecology. "How is that possible?"

"That's just how life developed here. Doran could explain, but he doesn't speak English."

No animal life? "How did you all come about?" Before Tira could answer, Fern figured it out. "I bet you came here the same way I did."

"That's right."

"Where from?"

Tira didn't answer. They had come to a clearing. She gestured around and said, "This is our village."

On the bank of a small river sat a semi-circle of a dozen or so thatched houses. Most were oval with rounded roofs and an awning in front of the only door. None had windows. "This is where you live?"

Tira nodded.

"No electricity or anything?"

"No. We get along quite well without it." Tira led Fern to a house where Andli sat on a mat in the shade of the awning. She appeared to be spinning thread with a hand-held device. At their approach, she smiled and said, "Salut."

"That means 'hello.'"

"Salut," Fern said.

A few children peeked around the side of the house. Tira spoke to them, indicated Fern, and said her name. The children twittered among themselves, repeating her name, but they kept adding a vowel, calling her "Ferna" or "Ferni."

Tira coaxed two girls to come forward. "These are my sisters, Tala and Ara."

Fern felt a pang. They were about the same ages as her own sisters.

"Salut." The girls ran off with their companions.

Tira introduced two larger children. "These are my brothers, Jorsil and Donal."

The boys said, "Salut."

Fern hadn't guessed they were boys. "Do girls and boys dress the same?" she asked. "And all have long hair?"

"Yes. That's our custom." Donal, the younger boy, left. Jorsil, who looked a little older than Fern, lingered behind. Fern caught him staring at her. With a timid smile, he touched his head. "He's admiring your hair," Tira said.

Tira gestured around the open area in the middle of the houses. "This is our *sameg*. The closest English word would be 'the common.' Each family has their own house, but we share our food."

They walked across the sameg to a stone structure that resembled a large barbecue pit. "This is where we cook." A waist-high wall of tightly fitted stones contained the fire. The wall curved like a sea shell, with an opening wide enough to let someone access the fire. Wide, flat stones made counter space. On one side rose a large chimney with ovens that smelled of baking bread. Several biscuits were stacked on the counter by the chimney. Clay pots of soup simmered by the fire. Tira pointed to another pot. "That's hot water for tea. And that," she indicated a large clay pot outside the fire pit, "is for cold water." Under the counter were stone shelves stacked with wooden cups and bowls, all engraved with designs and polished to a shine, some inlaid with colorful stones. Tira said, "Anytime you get hungry, you can find food here. But for now, eat only things you've already tried. Andli doesn't know if you'll have any reactions to our food, like your mother does, so she wants to introduce things one at a time."

"Where's the silverware?" Fern asked.

"We don't use any. Rina made spoons for you and your mother." Lifting a two-handled wooden jug, she said, "This is to haul water from the river." At the water's edge, a man squatted on a stone shelf, filling a similar jug. Tira pointed downstream to a rocky area. "That's where we wash things." A handful of people bent over the water, swirling articles of clothing in the current, singing to the rhythm of their motions.

Fern lifted her eyes to the surrounding country. Green hills rose above the trees, and beyond them, black mountains. No cropland was in sight, nor any other dwellings, and no smoke indicated other cooking fires. All she saw was wilderness. "How many of you live here?"

"About a hundred. And we have another village by the sea."

"How big is it?"

"About the same size."

Fern waited for Tira to tell her about other towns, perhaps cities, other countries.

Instead, Tira said, "That's all of us, except the walkers."

"Walkers?"

"Those who are traveling on foot. The old people—once their children are grown and they've passed down all their knowledge—they can choose to leave home and explore the world."

"So, there are only a little over two hundred people on this whole planet?"

"That's right."

Fern scanned the horizon. Something about this unpeopled world thrilled her. "Where did you all come from? Why do you live here?"

Tira glanced around. A group of children had followed, keeping a shy distance. She whispered, "We came here to escape from the thortles."

"Thortles?"

"Shhh. That's what we call them. The English word would be something like 'captors.'"

Fern shivered. "Captors? They captured you?"

Tira nodded. "Actually, our ancestors. We've been here over a hundred years."

Fern glanced around. "So, where are those—whatever they are?"

"Oh, they're not here! They live on a different planet."

"You mean there's another world out there with people on it?"

"They're not really people. Not human, anyway."

"Then, what are they like?"

Tira held Fern's eyes. "Can you imagine a cockroach as big as you are?"

Fern cringed.

"Don't worry. They don't know where we are. We're safe here."

Fern looked up at the sky, blue with patches of clouds and a sun much like her own. Did danger lurk beyond that innocent sky? "Why would they want to capture you? Do they eat people?"

"No, thank goodness, they're herbivores. They used us as slaves." She looked at the nearby children. "Let's not talk about them." Tira was quiet for a moment. "We're not one hundred percent sure where we came from originally, but we think we came from Earth. Our people are the same as yours. We can even breed with people from your world."

Fern blushed. "You breed with people on Earth?"

"What? No. Not often. We're curious about your people, that's why we go there. It's a safe place for us to visit."

Fern remembered her old dreams of becoming an astronaut. She never thought she'd visit another planet this way. She thought of the moons she'd seen the night before.

Moons. The night sky. Something had changed. Last night she'd experienced no fear of the stars! When had she last viewed the night sky without feeling prey to some unspeakable terror? What was different about last night? Was it because the unthinkable had finally happened? She'd been snatched from her home world and brought here. Had seeing Tira at Disney World triggered a premonition that initiated her fear of stars?

CHAPTER 5
NO RECOURSE

Fern's mind turned from the beauty of the world around her to the desolation within. She had lost everything. Her father was dead. She was separated from her sisters and all else she'd known by an impossible distance. All she had left was her mother. Fern yearned to be cradled in her mother's arms like an infant, to be assured that she was safe, that all was well. But Mama was sick, and Fern didn't know how to help her.

Jorsil, who'd been standing nearby, spoke in his language.

Tira interrupted Fern's thoughts. "Jorsil's going swimming. Do you want to go, too?"

Without thinking, Fern said, "Sure."

They lead her on a path along the river, through the woodland. The children following them filtered into the forest. A few scrambled up trees. The child in Fern longed to join them. Would anyone object to a girl her age climbing a tree?

They came to a warm stream that flowed toward the river. Tira said, "This is the one by your hut. The water's rich in minerals and has healing properties. That's why we built the house there. Andli's been bathing your mother in it, and it seems to help." They waded across.

The woods opened to a field covered by the same low, spreading plant that grew near the hut. Here the river widened into a small lake. A roaring sound caught Fern's attention. "What's that?"

Tira smiled and said, "Come on."

They ran to the edge of a cliff where the lake spilled over and cascaded some fifty feet down to a pool. Fern was captivated by the sight. From the pool, the river descended over steep rapids into a thickly wooded vale. Her eyes followed its course to where it bent behind a shoulder of the mountain. Then she focused on the ridge across the way. Stony outcroppings jutted from among the trees. Ravines cut into the slopes. A forested peak rose on the other side of the crest. Beyond that—mountain after mountain after mountain, into the blue distance.

"Hang on to your hat," Tira said as a gust of wind blew up the river.

Fern drank in the breathtaking scene, but something was missing—flowers—she saw none, anywhere.

Tira broke the spell. "Let's go swimming."

Fern waded into water as warm as a Florida lake in summer. She closed her eyes and, for a moment, imagined she was at home. The water lapped against the hem of her tunic. "Oh, I don't have a bathing suit."

"You don't need one," Tira said.

Jorsil stripped off his tunic, and he wore nothing underneath. Immediately, Fern turned away. Tira laughed and said something to Jorsil, who jumped into the water.

"It's okay, you can turn around now. I'm sorry. I forgot you're not used to skinny dipping. That's how we swim here."

Fern glared at Tira and turned carefully. Jorsil stood chest deep in the lake, a puzzled expression on his face. "Doesn't anyone wear underwear here?" Fern muttered.

"Not really. It isn't needed. We wouldn't wear clothes at all except that we need to protect our skin from the sun, and from getting scratched in the woods."

It was all too much. Fern scrunched her eyes to keep from crying. "I don't want to go swimming now."

Tira said nothing for a moment. Then, "When the sun is high, we swim in our clothes to keep from getting sunburned. Maybe you could swim then. Or I could ask Taran to arrange a time for you. Would you object to other girls being naked?"

Fern didn't care if she ever went swimming again. And she didn't want special treatment. She only muttered, "I don't know."

They walked back toward the village. Jorsil caught up with them, fully clothed, and spoke to Tira. She answered. Jorsil shrugged and went his way. Tira said, "I told him why you reacted the way you did when he took off his clothes. He didn't know your people object to nakedness. And I do apologize. I'd forgotten."

Fern thought of Andli, who probably had never gone to Earth, yet she had been sensitive to Fern's need for privacy. But Tira, who should know better, managed to embarrass both her and Jorsil. They returned to the sameg in silence.

People were gathering around the fire pit. Tira introduced Fern to a few, identifying them as aunts, uncles, or cousins.

"Is everyone here related?"

"Yes. It's unavoidable. We're all cousins to some degree. It's hard to find a mate who isn't closely related."

A mate? Fern shook her head. Was Tira one of those girls who thought about nothing but boys?

A man pulled a platter of biscuits from an oven. Another platter, freshly baked, sat on the counter. Rina ladled soup into bowls. She greeted Fern with a smile.

By the angle of the sun, Fern estimated it was late morning, but she was hungry.

As if she read Fern's mind, Tira said, "We can eat anytime we want to, but most of us are hungry by this time of day. Afterwards, it gets hotter. Then we rest, take naps, and go to school."

"School? Where's the school?"

"Everywhere. Taran will start your lessons soon. Everyone is a teacher. After you learn our language, it'll be easier for you."

Fern thought about school and friends back on Earth. She hadn't quite grasped the notion that she was stuck here for the rest of her life. What about her future? She'd always wanted to go to college, to do something that would make a difference in the world. Were those plans permanently derailed? Yet another loss added to her burden. How could she live like this for the rest of her life? She sighed, and it turned into a yawn.

"Are you tired?" Tira asked. "I'm not surprised. The days are longer than on Earth, about twenty seven hours." She dipped a bowl of soup from a smaller pot and handed it to Fern.

"I want to go back to my mother. Can I take my food there?"

"Sure."

"Can I take some to her, too?"

Tira hesitated. "She hasn't been able to eat, but you can try. If she could drink water, that would be the best thing." Tira dished out a second bowl, picked up two biscuits, and gave Fern one. "I'll take you back, but you're free to go anywhere you like, whenever you like. There's little danger here, except—be careful of too much sun. And lightning storms. After midday, it's safe to go out in the open, but don't forget your hat. You're always safe under the trees, unless it's storming."

On the way to the hut, Fern said, "I wish I had a book to read."

"Taran will teach you how to do that."

The day was growing hot, yet it was comfortable inside the hut. Fern's mother slumped over in the rocking chair, looking small and old. She squirmed to a sitting position when the girls entered. They set the food on the table.

To Fern, Tira said, "I'll come for you later, if you like."

"Okay."

Fern slid a bowl and biscuit across the table. "Mama, these are for you."

"Thank you, Fern, but I can't eat."

Fern wasted no time finishing her lunch. Then she dipped the remaining bread into Mama's soup and offered it to her. "Taste this. It's good."

Her mother bit off a few crumbs. "Yes. It is." But no sooner had she swallowed than she began choking, grabbed a towel, and retched into it. Almost nothing came up.

"I'm sorry." Fern handed her a cup of water. "Maybe you should drink something first."

Her mother dipped a corner of the towel into the water and cleaned her mouth. "It's no use. It's the same. I can't eat or drink. I'm just not going to make it."

That remark didn't register on Fern. She had seldom seen her mother sick. "I thought they gave you some medicine."

"Yes, but it's not enough. You see, Fern, this place, this planet, is actually poisonous to human beings. In order to live here, your body chemistry has to be altered. They helped you do that, but it didn't work for me. The food, the water, even the air, is toxic to me."

"I don't remember altering my body chemistry."

"You were unconscious. They took us down to the creek and covered us with mud. Lila explained that our bodies needed to be repopulated with local microorganisms. Kind of like after we take antibiotics. But there's more. Since we evolved independently of the plants here, our bodies don't recognize them as food. And to make it more complicated, the orientation of molecules here is right-handed. On Earth, most are left-handed." She had to catch her breath and moisten her mouth. "Andli and Doran and some others—I don't know exactly what they were doing. It looked like they were praying over us. Anyway, they fixed things in your body so you could live here. But they couldn't fix me." She bent over the bowl of hot rocks and inhaled the vapor. "I don't know how much longer I can hold on." She gave Fern a weak smile. "These are good people. You'll be safe here with them."

What was she saying? "No! You can't die! We have to do something."

"They've done everything they can."

"Then we have to get you back to Earth."

"They tried. They couldn't do it."

"*I'll* do it. If I brought you here, I can take you back."

"But you don't know how. Even if you did, could you change your body chemistry back? If you couldn't, then *you* would die."

"But back home, they could give me some medicine for it."

"No, Fern, there is nothing the doctors on Earth can do for this. I know these things. I also know…" With difficulty, she cleared her throat. "Even though these people appear to be primitive, they are anything but. They have medical skills I never dreamed of. I don't understand how, but they've made it possible for me to breathe. And not just with this." She indicated the imbwina bowl. "I should have suffocated before now. I should feel more pain. If we had their skills on Earth…" She shook her head and breathed more vapor. "Fern, don't ask me why, but I think you belong here." She held out her arms. "It will be all right. I can go in peace. I can be with your father." Her eyes squinted, as though holding back tears, but none fell. "I'm sorry about last night. I was angry with Daddy. I'm only human. But I still love him dearly, Fern, and I miss him desperately." She folded her arms around Fern and held her for several minutes.

Fern whispered, "I need to go to the latrine." Instead, she returned to the village to seek Taran. Andli and Rina were eating lunch in front of Tira's house. Fern said, "Taran?" They pointed across the river. Fern had no idea how to find him there, so she asked for Tira, and the women pointed toward the lake.

Tira and several other youths were swimming, fully clothed this time. Fern swam to Tira. "Where's Taran?"

"He's—I don't know how to tell you. He'll be back tonight. Why?"

Tonight might not be soon enough. "I need him to help my mother."

Tira stopped to tread water. "What's wrong?"

"She's dying." Fern swallowed the lump in her throat. "We've got to get her back to Earth."

"That's been tried."

"*I* haven't tried. I'll take her back."

Tira shook her head. "Do you know how?"

"I brought her here, didn't I?"

Tira swam to shore and Fern followed.

"I'll send a message to Taran and ask him to hurry back. Then you can talk to him. I'm going home now to take a nap." They returned to the village. Before entering her house, Tira took off her wet tunic and draped it over the edge of the awning. Fern averted her eyes, but not before she observed, with some satisfaction, that Tira's breasts were smaller than hers.

Fern made it only halfway back to the hut. She sagged to the ground, leaned against a tree, and burst into tears. Her heart hung like a heavy stone in the bottom of her chest. She missed her father. She couldn't imagine life without him. She missed her sisters, too. At least they were safe.

A horrible thought drove that certainty from her mind. She had lowered them to the ground but didn't know for sure what happened to them afterward. Had they reached a neighbor's before they froze to death? She had pushed those thoughts from her mind, but now they rushed back. Another horrible thought—if she were able to save her mother, would she lose her own life? If she did, and her sisters were dead, what would Mama do then? Was there no right course of action? All this was beyond her capacity for worry at the moment. She pushed those thoughts back and locked them in a dark corner of her mind.

Tears slowly dried. The tree trunk cradled her back. She imagined strong arms around her and looked up. Branches covered with heart-shaped leaves dipped gently in a soft breeze. Such a friendly tree. In a way, she wished she could spend a little time here before she returned home. How many people on Earth had set foot on another planet?

She stood and brushed off her tunic. It was nearly dry. She returned to the hut. Mama smiled weakly but didn't question her absence. Fern ate her mother's untouched lunch and lay down for a nap.

Another thunderstorm gave relief from the afternoon heat. After the storm passed, Fern went to the sameg and found Taran. "I need you to help me go back to Earth, and take my mother with me."

"We would have already done that, were it possible."

"But she's dying. If she could go back to Earth, she'd be all right, wouldn't she?"

"Very likely. Do you understand why your mother is dying?"

"Yes. Something about body chemistry. You changed mine but couldn't change hers."

He nodded. "It's not entirely that simple, but you have the idea. If wrashiru were successful, if you were able to take your mother back, you'd need to change your body chemistry again, or you'd die the same way your mother is dying now."

"I know. I want to try anyway."

He studied her for a few minutes. Finally, he nodded. "All right. There are no guarantees, but we can try. Some of us are adept at guiding wrashiru. We'll give it a try tonight."

Taran accompanied Fern back to the hut and explained the plan to Fern's mother.

She said, "I will not permit it. Right now all my children are alive. I will not risk Fern's life. I'd rather die myself."

"I know. It probably won't work, but Fern has a right to try. We'll do all we can to keep her safe."

She shook her head. "It doesn't matter. It's not going to work."

CHAPTER 6
ONE LAST PLEASANT EVENING

After Taran left, Fern braced herself for an argument. Instead, after long moments of awkward silence, her mother said, "Fern, I'd like to go to the village for a while. I'll need help. Will you bring someone?"

"Yes, ma'am." Fern hurried to the sameg. Tira stood at the fire pit mixing dough, singing quietly to herself. Fern told Tira what she needed.

Tira called to Andli and Rina, who accompanied Fern to the hut. The women walked on each side of Fern's mother, supporting her, while Fern followed with the rocking chair. The woods were still wet from rain, yet the ground within the circle of houses was dry.

Fern set the chair under the awning of Tira's house. The women sat on mats and took up work. Rina was carving designs on a bowl using an implement with a shiny black blade. Andli picked up a cylindrical frame strung with thread and began weaving.

Fern sat down, awkwardly, trying not to expose her private parts. She'd noticed Andli and Rina had gracefully seated themselves without embarrassment and now sat cross-legged, the hems of their tunics making a modest dip between their legs.

Mama gestured towards Andli. "That's a loom, and she's making a tunic for one of her grandparents."

"Oh." Fern didn't know such looms existed.

The two women began to sing in unison. Fern wondered how closely related they were. Rina stood taller than Andli, but her eyes were almost the same shade as Tira's. Fern would have thought she was Taran's sister if Tira hadn't grouped her among the cousins.

Tira joined them and said to Fern, "Andli will make you a new tunic when she finishes this one. The one you're wearing belonged to a cousin. We didn't have any spare ones your size. Your mother has an old one of Rina's."

Fern didn't mention that she was going home and wouldn't need a new tunic. She looked down at what she wore. For a hand-me-down, it was in good condition, but it didn't fit well, being too baggy. The color was hardly faded, but it was yellow, which didn't become her. The one her mother wore was much nicer, blue-green with golden designs embroidered around the neck and sleeves. Fern's eyes wandered to the doorway of the house. From what she could see, it was fancier than their hut.

Rina spoke to Tira.

"You can come inside." Tira led Fern into the house. The front room had no furniture, only four pallets on the floor, covered with colorful cloth. Floor and walls were covered with woven mats. Baskets of various sizes and shapes hung by the beds. Beside them sat larger baskets with folded cloth peeking above the brim and, next to one, something that looked like a tree stump, the top covered with cloth. The fabrics were colorful, woven with beautiful designs, and even the baskets had dyed cords worked into them. There were no windows, but a space between the walls and roof let in light and air. The posts that supported the roof were intricately carved with vines and leaves and designs unfamiliar to Fern. She fingered a carving. "It's beautiful."

Curtains of heavy cloth, embroidered with pictures of mountains and trees, hung in the doorways in the back of the room. Tira took Fern through the door on the left into a smaller room. Three pallets lay on the floor and baskets hung on the walls. "This is where my sisters and I sleep. The other room is for my brothers, but Jorsil is old enough to sleep on the sameg, so he doesn't always sleep here. My parents sleep in the main room."

Fern wondered why there were four beds in the parents' room, but her attention was drawn to a couple of rag dolls tucked under the blankets of two beds. She smiled. That was the same way her sisters put their dolls to bed, and she had done the same when she was younger. She sighed. Those dolls had been consumed by the fire.

Tira let her peek into the boys' room. It was the same as the girls'. A mandolin hung on the wall and, to Fern's surprise, one of those beds also had a doll.

"Why don't you have furniture?"

"We don't need it. It's healthy to sit on the floor, and the beds are comfortable."

"Why do my mother and I have cots? And where did the rocking chair come from?"

"We wanted you to be comfortable until you were used to our ways. Lila's sons, who live in the village by the sea, built the rocking chair. Andli thought it would give your mother comfort, and it has."

"You call your mother by her first name?"

"Yes. And we don't need last names, there are so few of us."

Children had gathered around the rocking chair. Curious fingers crept under the rockers. Fern's mother stopped rocking and smiled at them. From time to time, the three women smiled at one another. Andli's presence seemed especially comforting.

"Mama," Fern said, "down this river there's a lake, and a waterfall…"

"I know. While you were unconscious, before I lost my strength, I walked about. I didn't want to miss my chance to see a new planet, even if I couldn't tell anyone back home about it. Lila stayed with me and told me a lot about this place and these people before she went home." She had to moisten her mouth and catch her breath. "You'll learn all in time. This place is truly beautiful. I wish I could stay longer and enjoy it."

They spent several peaceful hours watching the activities on the sameg. Men and women sat under their awnings, engaged in craft work or fixing children's hair. Men and women alike had long, dark hair, elaborately plaited. Men's beards were also braided. Everyone wore colorful tunics that reached to the knees, belted with elaborately decorated straps. Most were barefoot, but a few wore sandals. All articles of clothing were embroidered or had designs woven into the fabric. A woman, whose tunic opened in front, openly nursed a baby. Fern felt like she was in a scene from a *National Geographic* magazine, but a subtle aura of sophistication belied this impression. As her mother said, these people were not as primitive as they appeared. And Tira and Taran spoke good English and had visited Earth.

Everyone Fern saw was attractive, with regular features and good teeth, none too fat or too thin. Even those with touches of gray hair stood straight and looked youthful. The only deformity she saw was a prominent scar on one man's face. Despite this, he was handsome and dignified. Fern looked down at her ill-fitting tunic and felt shabby by comparison.

She watched people bring firewood to the sameg and prepare food. Everyone sang while they worked. In one corner of the sameg stood a tetherball pole. Instead of a round ball, a stuffed sack dangled on the rope. Just outside the circle of houses, children played a game that resembled soccer. Fern didn't notice any disagreements. Other than the dolls, she saw no toys.

The strange language fascinated Fern. Some words were soft, almost melodious, but others had harsh sounds that reminded her of metal pieces coming into contact, clicking, sliding, or grinding against one another.

She and her mother stayed through supper, which was the same as breakfast, lunch, and meals in between. Fern longed for meat. Tira's family, as well as Rina and Doran, joined them under the awning for supper. Doran didn't closely resemble either Taran or Andli. Shorter than Taran and beardless, he looked almost Asian. Although they conversed in their language, Taran spoke in English and occasionally translated what others said.

Fern's mother didn't eat, but she expressed curiosity about the food. "What do you call the bread?"

Tira answered, "Skri. And the soup is kirrib."

After supper, as the sky began to darken, the villagers built a fire in the center of the sameg and gathered around it, sitting on mats. Fern's mother asked for her rocking chair to be moved into the circle. She could barely walk. Once settled, she smiled, moistened her mouth, and said, "I've always thought it curious, human beings' love of fire. It's something atavistic in us. A campfire, a hearth fire, even a candle will hold our fascination and give us comfort." Her face sobered. "It holds our attention like a TV does. Even when it's not a necessity, when we have electricity." Her voice grew rough. "We didn't need that fireplace. Even when the electricity was out, we had gas. We would have survived. Just something we thought we wanted."

Fern cringed.

The activity on the sameg diverted her attention. Those who'd worn no ornamentation during the day now donned colorful necklaces, bracelets, and anklets. A few young people let down their hair. Some brought out musical instruments—string, wind, and percussion—made of wood, carved with pictures and designs. Rina sat among the musicians, holding the curious cloth-covered stump Fern had seen in the house. Soon people were singing and dancing. A small group acted out a skit that made everyone laugh. Even though they couldn't understand the words, Fern and her mother laughed, too.

Taran stood up and began to talk. He gestured with his hands as though describing something. Tira joined him and he motioned to the musicians. Someone plucked a chord and a wind instrument picked up the tune. It sounded familiar. Taran and Tira began to sing, "Oh, give me a home/ Where the buffalo roam…." Fern laughed and her mother smiled with delight. When they sang the lines, "How often at night/When the heavens are bright/With the light of the glittering stars…," Fern looked up at the stars, grateful that they no longer frightened her. For a fleeting moment, she almost felt at home.

Other songs followed. When one haunting tune was played, Mama whispered, "I can't remember the name of this one, but it's from somewhere on Earth. It's in the minor key." A few of the dances seemed vaguely familiar. The first time a sweaty dancer sat down near Fern, she instinctively recoiled, until she noticed the woman didn't smell bad. How did they control body odor in this climate? Maybe by swimming several times a day.

One moon, then the other, rose beyond the trees. Fern glanced at her mother, who gazed at the moons, her face aglow in their light. Then Mama lowered tired eyes and asked to be taken back to the hut. When she tried to stand, her legs collapsed and she would have fallen if Fern hadn't caught her. Taran and Doran carried her in the chair and Rina accompanied them.

The music continued. Fern looked back at the sameg, reluctant to leave, but determined to go home. She turned away and asked Taran, "Are you going to help me?"

"As long as you understand there are no guarantees."

"I understand."

In the hut, he sat on the empty cot and talked to Fern's mother, who was too weak to protest. "I have one request," she said. "When...*if* Fern arrives back on Earth, if she cannot adjust, I want her brought back here. I do not want my child losing her life for a fool's errand. I'm ready to die." She had to moisten her mouth. "I'm actually looking forward to being with my soul mate again."

Taran nodded. "We'll do all we can to ensure Fern's safety."

"Fern, do you promise me that? That you'll come back if you need to?"

Fern hadn't considered the stark possibility that she and her mother could be permanently separated. "Yes, ma'am." She hugged Mama as though this were their last embrace.

Rina handed Fern some tea. Taran said, "This will help relax your mind and body."

The tea made her need to use the latrine. When she went down to the warm stream to wash her hands, she looked around one more time. This place was so beautiful. Her thighs ached from a day of climbing uphill and down, but she loved the mountains. She wished she'd had time to explore the waterfall. Moonlight filtered through the tree tops. Two moons! How her father would have loved to see this. She began to cry. Even if she could safely take herself and her mother back home, there would be this big hole in their lives. But she had crossed the universe to save Mama. It didn't make sense to let her die now.

CHAPTER 7
WRASHIRU

Fern tried to prepare herself mentally for wrashiru. The calming tea eased her trepidation. By the time she returned to the hut, her mother was settled comfortably in her chair.

Taran said, "I will guide both of you into a hypnotic trance. If you have any disturbing visions or sensations, don't panic. You'll be safe, and getting upset might disrupt the process. Rina will join us and others will support us mentally. If wrashiru is successful, you'll find yourselves at the home of some of our people who live in Pennsylvania. Their names are John and Alice Devoir. When you arrive, you'll be naked and disoriented. They'll know how to help you." He and Rina sat on the floor, and Fern took her place by the rocking chair. "Holding hands is not necessary to the process, but it supports us mentally," Taran said. Everyone joined hands. "Let's close our eyes."

Fern gently squeezed her mother's hand. Taran's soothing voice guided them. Fern began to relax, then to focus inward. Soon she found herself following not his words, but the images they evoked. Slowly, the images faded, leaving only a heightened awareness.

Music filled the periphery of her mind. Voices sang words she didn't understand. The songs gave way to murmuring, such as one hears in church when hundreds of voices are saying the same prayer. Then all came together, one voice, one note, stretched out into time and distance.

Fern imagined herself walking out of the hut, leading her mother by the hand, down the slope to the stream. They waded into the water, deeper and deeper, until they were completely submerged. The warm liquid gave comfort, as in a womb. She surrendered to the experience.

* * *

Fern stood barefoot on the cold sand in front of the charred remains of her home. She recognized the site only by the surrounding trees and the brick steps which lead to a chaos of tin roofing twisted among concrete foundation supports. To one side rose a brick monument to dashed hopes and dreams—the fireplace and chimney. Fern could smell the water-damp ash. The century-old azaleas were reduced to dust, the majestic oak trees half-burned, and the magnolia that had stood outside her bedroom window, a charred snag.

She stepped through the barrier of yellow tape, climbed the steps, and scanned the ruins for anything familiar. Almost nothing remained. She raised her eyes to where the second story had been and let them roam to where her room once existed. Nothing but air. She closed her eyes and recalled pleasant days sitting on her bed, reading, dreaming. Days that were gone forever.

She opened her eyes and allowed her gaze to drift down the chimney and settle on the hearth where she had last seen her father. In her mind's eye, she pictured him sitting there, relaxing. A snarled knot of metal lay on the ground. The fireplace screen? If only she'd said something...

She refused to let her imagination carry the scene further. The fat-rich pine that had resisted rot and termites for a hundred years had fulfilled its other purpose. It had burned. Too well.

Beyond the trees, frost on the cabbage fields sparkled in the morning sun. The loveliness of the scene was lost on her. Fern turned away.

She found herself in the warm comfort of her grandparents' living room. The sound of voices led her to the kitchen where her little sisters sat at the breakfast table. Fern nearly laughed with relief and joy. The girls were safe!

Her grandmother was on the phone. "Please don't transfer me to another person. I'm calling long distance. I'm just trying to get school records so

I can put these girls in school." After a pause, "No I don't have any custody papers. Their parents both died in a fire, and we just had the funeral yesterday. These girls need to be in school. No, I don't have a death certificate yet." She swallowed a sob. "I can show you the newspaper clippings if you need proof." After another pause, she grumbled, "Oh, thank you," and hung up.

Her grandfather entered through the back door.

"This is an awful mess," Grandma said. "What do they think—we kidnapped these children?"

He answered in a low voice. "They don't need to hear you talking like this. They've been through enough already."

"Haven't we all." She collapsed into a chair and her eyes watered. "But look at them. They're paying no attention."

Fern looked at her little sisters, playing a silly game with each other instead of eating. She smiled. No one seemed to notice her, so she spoke. "Grandma? Grandpa?" Her grandmother looked her way, but didn't answer.

"I'm so glad to see you," Fern said, stepping forward to give her a hug. But her arms went right through her! Fern looked at her arms in disbelief. Her grandmother ignored her, stood up, and walked away. *What's wrong? Can't they see me?*

Fern now realized she was not naked, nor where she expected to be, and her mother was not with her.

Grandma pulled a tissue out of a box and wiped her eyes. "I'm going to miss them so much," she said. "Especially Fern. She had so much potential, so much to look forward to."

"But I'm here!" Fern almost shouted. "Can't you hear me?" She felt tears flowing down her cheeks.

Grandpa cleared his throat and, in a thick voice said, "She really showed her mettle. Rescuing her sisters, then going back for her parents like that. This world has lost a true hero."

Fern didn't feel like a hero. *They think I'm dead. I don't know how to tell them I'm not.*

Nevertheless, she stayed with them for hours, watching her sisters play and her grandparents go about daily tasks. Their very existence nourished her soul.

After lunch, the children were put down for a nap. Fern sat on the bedside and talked to them. She told them she and Mama were still alive, but on another world far away. She explained that Mama was sick and may have to go stay with Daddy in Heaven. She tried to say things that would comfort them. She tried to hug them. "I love you," she said.

Then Fern heard a voice calling her name and turned around. She was no longer in her grandparents' house, but lying on her cot in the thatched hut an eternity away. Rays of the rising sun filtered through the trees. Her mother sat in the rocking chair and Taran and Rina remained seated on the floor.

Fern sat up. "What happened?"

"Well," Mama drawled, "we didn't go back to Earth."

"I did." She felt like Dorothy returning from Oz. She told them all that had transpired. "It was real, it wasn't a dream."

Her mother cried tearlessly through the telling. "You fell asleep and we thought the wrashiru had failed. But you may have been astral traveling." She had to wet her mouth. "That's another thing I didn't believe in, but now I'm not so sure. If it was a real experience, then we know the girls are okay, are going to be okay."

"I felt like I was really there, but no one could see me or hear me, and I couldn't touch anything. Everybody was sad, but they're okay. They're safe."

Mama closed her eyes and smiled. "I'll be able to rest now."

"But why didn't the wrashiru work? I really tried. Why couldn't we go back?"

Her mother said, "Some things are not meant to be."

Taran asked, "How many hours do you think you spent there?"

Fern counted in her mind. Breakfast, lunch, nap time. "Four, at least. Maybe five, or six?"

He nodded. "You maintained your trance state well into the night, then you fell asleep on the floor and we put you to bed. Rina and I stayed here to be sure you were all right. It was no dream. You weren't able to take your physical body back to Earth, but you were able to visit in what you'd call your astral, or etheric body. We call this 'ethenos.'"

Fern nodded. "It's strange. I knew I wasn't in my real body, but the thought never crossed my mind that I might be dead, a ghost." She lowered her eyes. "Mama, at first I didn't even notice you weren't with me."

Taran said, "You were completely focused on the experience, to the exclusion of anything else."

Fern turned to him. "Even though I couldn't go back the way I wanted to, I'm grateful for your help. At least I saw my sisters. Will I be able to do that again?"

"Apparently you have that ability." Taran and Rina rose. "We need to rest. We'll send you some breakfast."

After they left, Mama said, "Tell me more about the girls, and your grandparents. How did they look?"

Fern related every detail she could remember.

Her mother listened with closed eyes and a smile that emanated peace. When Fern finished, she said, "I almost feel like I was there with you."

CHAPTER 8
GOODBYE

Andli and Tira brought breakfast for Fern and fresh imbwina for her mother. "After you eat, come join us at the village," Tira said.

Breathing the vapor added more color to Mama's face and briefly renewed Fern's hope. But she still couldn't stand up. "Please don't worry about me, Fern. I'll soon be with your father. Taran and Andli will take you in and raise you. They are good people. They'll love you like I do." She wet her mouth. "Customs are different here. It'll be strange for a while, but you'll get used to their ways." She sighed. "I have so much I wish I could tell you, but I haven't enough breath. Maybe someday you'll be able to go back to Earth and tell your sisters what happened."

Fern didn't know what to say. She really liked Andli, and she respected Taran, but how could they replace her parents? How could she accept Tira as a sister? And Tira's sisters and brothers—if only she could be with her own sisters, and her grandparents. She wanted to cry, but it was as though she had been wrung dry of all her tears.

"Fern, eat your breakfast. You'll feel better."

Kirrib and skri. Soup and bread. Again. "Grandma made bacon, eggs, and toast," she said. "I wish I could've had some." She soaked the biscuit in the soup and managed to down the resulting mush. Then she lay down on her cot.

"Aren't you going to the village?"

"No. I'll stay here with you."

"Fern, go. I'll be fine. Come back and tell me what you see. I wish I could go with you."

With this mission Fern left the hut, but not for the village. Instead, she followed the stream uphill, hoping to find its source. The water grew warmer as she climbed, so she knew it was fed by a hot spring. But her flatlander legs soon tired and her bare feet, used to sand, began hurt from walking on roots and stones. Reluctantly, she turned back and descended to the crest of a hillock above their hut. Here, the ground was soft and nearly level, and the woods invited her in. As she drank in the sights and smells, awareness struck her—she lacked any fear of getting lost in this vast wilderness. Somehow, she felt at home, safe.

Not knowing her way back to the hut didn't trouble her. She walked downhill until she heard the sounds of the village and was able to get her bearings. Then she listened for the stream and found the path.

Back at the hut, Mama said, "Will you help me get into bed?"

As Fern supported her those few steps from chair to cot, she noticed how thin her mother had become, light enough to be almost no burden. Fern helped her get comfortable and covered her with a light blanket.

"Tell me what you found."

Fern described the warm stream. "Someday, I'll go all the way to the spring. I bet you could cook in it."

Her mother laughed, then caught her side as though it hurt. "Tell me more."

Fern described trees that reminded her of certain ones on Earth and other plants that were entirely foreign. "But I didn't see a single flower."

"I know. There aren't any bees or anything for them to attract. I didn't have the time to study the biology of this world. Doran probably has, but he doesn't speak English. Maybe you can learn all that for me."

Fern's stomach growled.

"Why don't you go eat lunch?" She held out her arms and Fern bent down to hug her. "I love you, Fern."

"I love you, too."

"Go, now. I will be fine."

When Fern reached the sameg, Tira greeted her, holding a basket. "Would you like some salad for lunch?"

"Salad?" Fern didn't see any by the fire pit.

"We'll go gather it. Our word for salad greens is 'lenitrus.'" She led Fern into the woods in the opposite direction of the lake.

Fern looked around for a garden but saw only forest. "Where do you grow your food?"

"It grows in the woods. That's one reason our village is here. There are lots of edible plants." Tira began to pluck some spear-shaped leaves and put them in the basket. Before picking a leaf, she would pause as though examining it.

"Didn't someone say I shouldn't eat anything I haven't already tried, to be sure I'm not allergic?"

Tira nodded. "We've been putting these in your tea and soup, so we know they're safe." She held up a leaf. "These are called rambit."

"I guess you don't have any meat here."

"No." Tira laughed.

Fern watched Tira pick a frilly, light green leaf, not unlike lettuce, so she started to gather more from a neighboring plant. Something nudged her mind and she felt a momentary distress.

"Wait!" said Tira.

Fern looked at the leaves in her hands. "What's wrong?"

Tira faced the plant and bowed her head for a few seconds. Then she answered, "We always ask permission before taking something from a living plant, then we give thanks to it afterwards. I apologized to this one and explained that you didn't know better. These are called wispis."

Asking permission from a plant? Fern had her doubts, but, as her father used to say, "When in Rome..." Although she felt foolish, she asked and thanked the next wispis plant she picked from.

Once they'd filled the basket, Tira said, "How about some salad dressing?" At the river bank, Tira spoke silently to a vine and dug a fat tuber from the soil beneath it. She washed it in the river and took it back to the fire pit where she crushed it into paste, using a stone that fit nicely in her hand. Then she mixed some dried herbs with the paste, poured half the contents of the basket into a large bowl, and scooped a hefty dollop of the dressing onto the lenitrus. "Will you dish up two bowls of kirrib and carry them to the house?"

"What about bowls for the salad?"

"We'll share it." She laid several skri on top.

Although quite hungry, Fern wasn't keen on eating from the same dish as Tira, but that was a lot of lenitrus for two people. It turned out that the whole household shared the same bowl, dipping the leaves into the dressing. The flavors of the greens resembled lettuce and spinach, but the paste tasted more like a peppery guacamole.

A young man brought them more skri. He greeted the family, spoke to Tira, and smiled at Fern. Tira introduced him as Aldan. He appeared to be a little older than Jorsil and had a hint of moustache above his lips. Fern caught him eying her hair.

After lunch, Fern went to the hut to check on her mother. She was finally sleeping, breathing without effort. Maybe she would start to get better now. Upon her return to the village, Fern mentioned this to Tira, who frowned and went immediately to Andli, who hurried toward the hut. Although she heard no one call him, Fern saw Taran heading in the same direction. With building anxiety, she followed them.

Andli bent over Fern's mother, peered into her eyes, felt her pulse, and listened to her chest. She stood up and looked silently at Taran.

He took Fern's hands in his own and said, "You should understand that her sleep may not have the outcome you desire."

"Isn't sleep what she needs?" Her mother had a peaceful half-smile on her face. Other than being so thin, she looked fine.

"Sleep can be healing, but it's doubtful it will have that effect now. We'll do all we can, but don't expect her to get better."

After this, Fern refused to leave her mother's side. Andli brought her loom to the hut and sat with them most of the afternoon. Tira brought food and water. Doran eventually relieved Andli, and after him, Rina, and later, Taran. This went on all night. Fern fell asleep to the music and singing on the sameg.

She dreamed that she woke and found Mama standing by the bed, strong and healthy. They joined hands and walked together down to the stream, then waded across. At the top of the further bank, instead of dense woods, they found a sandy lane arched over by oak trees draped with Spanish moss which swayed in a gentle breeze. They ran down the lane to their house, now fully restored. The azaleas, blooming banks of pink and white, seemed to bow to them as they passed. Fern led her mother up the porch steps. Through the screen door she saw her father enter the living room from the other side. Her parents flew into each other's arms, and Fern was carried away by their joy.

Someone called her name. Fern turned and found herself back in the hut in the pre-dawn light. The joy she had felt a moment ago lingered, but she already missed her mother. Andli led Fern to her mother's side. To her surprise, Mama still breathed. Fern knelt by the bed and took her mother's hand. She laid her forehead on it and closed her eyes. Andli knelt beside Fern and put an arm around her. Fern heard a raspy breath escape from her mother's throat. Her last. Andli folded Fern in her arms.

CHAPTER 9
MOTHERLAND

Fern had never seen a dead person before. Not knowing what else to do, she remained by her mother's body. Andli, then Rina, sat with her. Over the hours the body cooled and stiffened and Fern began to be repulsed by it. She was reminded of the dead puppy her family once found by the road. When they couldn't locate the owner, they buried it. Fern had seen that puppy before, prancing about the neighborhood, happy and full of life, but when it died, its essence had vanished. She felt guilty associating that puppy with her mother. She felt even more guilty for wanting to be away from the lifeless body.

Taran came to her and said, "Fern, you no longer need to keep vigil." He led her away.

She allowed herself to be guided through the day. Food was offered, but she had no appetite. She watched the burial preparations with detachment. She sat with Andli and the elders next door while they wove a large oblong basket, softly singing plaintive airs. After the heat of the afternoon, Tira and her brothers and sisters lined the basket with leaves. Andli and Taran carried the basket to her mother's hut, and Fern followed.

She had only vague ideas of the customs of her own people, having never before experienced the death of someone close to her. They didn't wash the body or dress it, merely left it in the clothing it had worn, placed it in the basket, and covered it with fragrant leaves that reminded Fern of her grandmother's lavender sachets.

Doran and two other men joined them. They picked up the basket and carried it back to the sameg where a procession formed. Andli walked on one side of Fern, and Tira on the other. The whole village followed, singing softly on the way to the meadow by the lake. Not far from the edge of the cliff, a hole had been dug in the ground.

Tira apparently was familiar with death. "We also bury our dead. It enriches the soil and gives us claim to this land as our own. Burying your mother here makes this your 'mother-land.' We don't usually bury the clothing with the body, but we thought you'd want it this way."

Fern nodded. She had seen the effort Andli put into weaving a tunic and knew clothing should not be wasted, but she appreciated their affording her mother this dignity.

Tira continued, "We dig the graves here because the soil is deep. In other places it's too shallow and rocky. The people that live in the village by the sea bury their dead at sea. It accomplishes the same purpose."

Fern saw no other graves.

Tira answered her thought. "We don't mark the graves, because the person herself is no longer here. Taran said he'll do what he knows of your people's customs to give your mother a proper burial."

The men set the bier down at the graveside and Taran motioned to Fern. "You may say goodbye," he said.

Fern knelt down beside the basket. What was she expected to do? She glanced up. Tira was looking back in the direction of the village. Taran had lowered his eyes. Andli made eye contact with her and smiled sadly. *I guess it doesn't matter what I do.* Fern bent over and brushed some of the leaves from her mother's body. She touched her hands. Cold. Stiff. This was no longer her mother. She planted a quick kiss on the forehead and replaced the leaves. At last, she was able to release her tears.

In English, Taran said, "We are here to say goodbye to our sister and our mother whose spirit has now joined the Universe. Let her body now join this world which we love and which she thought to be beautiful. We will miss her physical presence, but her spirit will be with us always." He then spoke to the other men and they lowered the basket gently into the grave. The people of the village came one by one, carrying leaves which they let fall into the hole. Then one by one, each picked up a spade full of soil to throw on top of the leaves.

Fern shut her eyes, but she couldn't close her ears to the sound of the dirt dropping into the grave. Every shovelful fell on her heart. Something came into her hands—the wooden spade. She opened her eyes and looked at it in confusion. No one spoke. Fern turned to Taran who stood expectantly beside her. She couldn't partake in burying all she had left of her family. She shook her head and he took the spade from her.

After the grave was filled, hands restored the ground-covering over the disturbed soil. It was over. No one stirred, as though waiting for Fern. She said the only thing she could think of, "There are no flowers."

Taran paused a moment. Then he spoke to Doran, who took the wooden spade and walked off into the woods. Most of the people silently returned to the village, but Tira's family and Rina stayed. Fern didn't know what to do. Over the past few days, her mother's presence had cushioned the tremendous loss of all else she had known. Now what was left?

Doran emerged from the woods with a seedling tree which he planted on the grave. "We call this tree a 'miaven,'" Taran said. "The molecules of your mother's body will rise into the tree."

Fern smiled sadly. At least she would have something to connect her to home and family. She was grateful that these people were willing to depart from their usual customs to comfort her. She remembered what her mother had said. These were good people and they would take care of her. Fern helped Doran firm the soil around the newly planted tree. It felt good to do something. Jorsil appeared with a wooden jug of water and handed it to Fern. She said, "Thank you," and poured the water over the tree's roots. Then she stood up. "Thank you all, very much."

One by one, they hugged Fern. Fern allowed Andli to lead her back to the village.

After the evening meal, Fern bathed in the stream by the hut and went in as if to spend the night there. So empty. Even the dim light didn't mask her mother's absence. No one sat in the rocking chair or slept on the bed.

Fern sat on her cot, unable to cry. Then she heard Andli's soft step at the doorway. Andli took Fern in her arms and let her cry out her grief.

"I know you mean well," Fern said, "but you can never replace my mother." Andli placed something in Fern's hand. It was a small pouch on a string, woven with fine cords of many colors. Fern opened it. Inside she found an intricate medallion made of a soft, golden material. Andli touched her hair. Fern realized it had been made from a lock of hair—her mother's. She found more tears and threw her arms around Andli. "Thank you." Andli hung the pouch around Fern's neck, took her hand, and led her back to the sameg.

The villagers gathered as usual, but tonight there was no dancing. The music was soft and subdued. Stories were told. Although she couldn't understand the words, Fern suspected they were about other loved ones who had passed on. She told Tira she wanted to go to bed. Tira led her into her own room where another pallet had been prepared. Fern recognized her mattress from the hut. A basket hung on the wall beside it. Above it, on a hook, was her hat.

Tira gestured to the basket. "This is for you to keep your things in. We usually sleep naked, but you can do as you wish."

Fern found her comb and another borrowed tunic in the basket. She suspected Andli had taken care of these things for her.

"Goodnight, sister." Tira hugged her.

"Goodnight." Fern couldn't call her sister. Although she knew it was unreasonable, a part of her blamed Tira for her being here, for her mother's dying. She felt ashamed of these feelings, but she couldn't help herself.

CHAPTER 10
THE LONGEST DAY

Fern woke before dawn when she heard the household stirring. As she stretched, the herbal aroma of the mattress infused in her a sense of well-being. She opened her eyes and realized she was the only girl still in bed. The main room, too, was empty. Outdoors, the air was surprisingly chilly. On the sameg, several youths had just rolled up their bedding. Tira's brother Jorsil smiled at Fern when he brought his into the boys' bedroom.

Men as well as women were using the latrine, so Fern went into the woods to relieve herself. She resolved to find a time when she could use the latrine in privacy. Back at the sameg, the aroma of baking bread invited her to the fire pit where Rina and others were preparing breakfast. Rina pointed at a stack of leftover skri. "Thanks," Fern said. While she nibbled the biscuit, more villagers gathered, greeting one another. Fern answered their saluts with an awkward, "Salut." The skri was dry. Unsure how to ask for something to drink, she went down to the river and dipped water with her hands.

The sky gradually grew lighter. Silence overtook the sameg and everyone turned toward Fern. What had she done? She choked on a crumb and only then comprehended that no one was staring at her, but at the horizon behind her. She turned just as the sun peeked above the mountains. The whole village began to sing. Although she didn't understand the words, Fern was caught up in the power of the song. Once the sun stood apart from the horizon, the singing ceased. She sought out Taran. "What just happened?"

"We welcomed the sun and gave thanks for the new day. Later, I'll teach you the words."

In a corner of the sameg, a group was engaged in stretching exercises that reminded Fern of yoga. When a few stripped off their tunics and went into headstands, she averted her eyes and retreated to her mother's hut, trying to wipe the images of naked men and women from her mind. Her thoughts turned to home. She didn't belong here. It was all too strange. How she missed her family! Most of all, she missed her mother. She cried.

Afterwards, Fern washed her face in the stream and returned to the hut, wondering what to do next. Tira came to announce breakfast.

"Is everyone decent?" Fern asked.

Tira laughed. "Yes, everyone is dressed now."

"I don't think it's funny. Somebody needs to warn me when people are going to be naked."

Tira's face sobered. "I'm sorry. I know you aren't used to it. Just think about when clothes wouldn't be needed. Or would get in the way. Then you'll know when to close your eyes."

By now the family, including Rina and Doran, were eating in front of the house. Someone had brought breakfast for Fern—soup and skri, again. At least this skri was fresh.

After they finished, Andli had Fern sit down while she combed her hair. Rina joined her and they braided it. Her shoulder length hair must have posed a challenge. The women knitted their brows in puzzlement and seemed to debate how best to plait it.

Jorsil and Tala took care of the dirty dishes. Other household members, including Doran, aired out bedding, humming or singing as they worked. Taran paused to say, "Each morning after breakfast, we tidy the house before we move on to other chores. Everyone collects firewood and carries a vessel of water to the cistern every day, even the toddlers."

Finally, Andli and Rina finished Fern's hair and stood back to admire their handiwork. Fern could tell from their faces it looked pretty, if not stylish by her standards.

Rina went into the house and returned with a small instrument which she handed to Fern. It had a small black blade and an abrasive handle. Fern looked at it quizzically. Rina took it from her and held up a finger. Fern watched her clean and trim a fingernail with it before giving it back.

Tira said, "This is to clean and pare your nails with. Be careful, it's sharp."

Andli held up a twig with a frayed end.

"That's a toothbrush," Tira said. "We'll show you what bush it's from so you can make your own. Come, I'll show you how to use it."

Fern followed Tira into their room where Tira fished a similar stick out of her basket. She proceeded to clean her teeth while Fern squirmed. It was almost as bad as watching Tira use the latrine.

"You get the idea," Tira said. "Of course, you use water, just like you did back home." Tira put her toothbrush away and grabbed her hat. "Get yours. We're going to gather firewood."

Fern took this opportunity to ask Tira what they used for deodorant.

"Nothing. Our bodies have smells, but we don't perceive them as unpleasant. Our diet is part of it, of course. Haven't you noticed no one objects to you when you're sweaty?"

Fern had noticed, but she thought it was because she bathed several times a day.

They joined Doran and several children, including Tala and Ara, by the fire pit. Tira handed Fern a sling made of strong canvas and said, "This is for the wood. We collect it every day. Usually I'm on my own, but you need instruction, so I'm along to translate."

"How much instruction do you need to fetch firewood?"

"You need to know where to go. And we don't use living wood, only fallen branches and trees that have died."

Doran led them past the lake. Fern looked across the field to her mother's grave and the little miaven tree. *I need to water it*, she thought.

Doran and the children sang in unison as they walked. They skirted the cliff and walked into the woods, then down a slope into the valley. Fern heard the roar of the waterfall. *Now I know how to get there.*

They stopped by a stream to rest. Doran remained standing and began to talk.

"What's he saying?" Fern whispered to Tira.

"He's teaching the children about the tree we're sitting under. That's another thing about going into the woods with Doran. You always learn something."

Doran looked at them. Fern cringed—they'd been caught talking in class. But instead of ceasing to chat, Tira said, "This tree is an 'erguvon.'"

Fern looked up into the canopy and saw heart-shaped leaves, just like the tree she had cried under—when? Two days ago? She remembered how the tree had seemed to comfort her when she leaned against it.

Tira translated Doran's short lecture, but Fern only half-heard. There was so much to learn, not to mention a new language.

"I'd like to ask Doran why there are no flowers here."

Tira spoke to Doran, then to Fern. "There are, but they're not showy like on Earth."

Doran reached up, carefully pulled down a lower branch, and pointed to the center of a whorl of leaves. Fern stood for a closer look.

"This is a female flower," Tira said. "The sticky center is the equivalent of a pistil in your botany." Fern reached out to touch it. "Be careful," Tira admonished. "We don't want to damage anything."

Doran gently let the branch go.

"How do they get pollinated? I mean, there aren't any bees or anything."

"Wind, water, and some other interesting ways. We'll save that for later." Everyone rose. Rest time was over.

They followed the creek uphill to a tangle of fallen wood that had washed downstream in a torrent. Everyone bowed their heads briefly, as though in prayer. Then Doran, Tira, and Tala began breaking sticks into lengths that could be carried in the slings. "You can do this, too," Tira said. "Just be careful not to hurt anything living, like that," she pointed to a vine grow-ing among the dead branches. Before long, the slings were filled and the children hoisted them onto their backs. One little boy seemed to strain under his burden. Doran smiled and removed several sticks. Tira laughed. "Rondal thinks he's a man. He always tries to carry too much."

On the way home, they stopped twice to rest. Tira said, "We can go ahead if you want to. We don't have to wait for them."

"That's okay. Maybe the little ones will need help." Fern wouldn't admit she wasn't used to such hard work. She welcomed the slower pace and frequent breaks the younger children needed. When they reached the meadow, Fern set down her load. "I'm going to water the tree. Go on without me. I know the way." Jorsil had left the water jug by the miaven tree. As she headed to the lake with it, Doran nodded approvingly to her.

When she returned to the sameg, Fern deposited her wood on the pile near the fire pit and wondered what to do with the sling. A boy approached and spoke to her in his language. Then he took the sling and headed to the woods.

Tira called Fern over to a group of children, including her brother Donal, who sat under a tree with what looked like a basket of nuts. "Come help us shell them," Tira said.

"What are they?"

"Nuts."

Fern joined them. Donal sang a song as he worked and the others intoned the chorus. Fern fumbled with the hulls, and bits of nutmeat slipped through her fingers. Donal nudged her elbow and, rattling off something in his language, showed Fern the proper technique. Then he resumed singing, in rhythm with his hand movements. Fern's performance improved, but she couldn't work as fast as the others. She nibbled on a nut, but it was bitter. "What do you use them for?"

"Just about everything." Tira said. "They're the main ingredient in skri, and we also use the powder to thicken soup."

"They must taste better when they're cooked."

"Oh, yes. They're good roasted."

Fern helped Tira carry the nutmeats to the fire pit. "What's your word for nuts?"

"Nuts. Same as English."

Why did they use an English word?

Tira popped a few unshelled nuts into an oven. A man was grinding nutmeats with a stone, singing softly as he worked. Tira continued, "The flour from roasted nuts thickens our soup, but for bread dough, they have to be raw or it won't stick together."

A woman joined the man, mixed the flour with water and other ingredients in a crock, and set it near the ovens. Then she took dough from a similar crock and shaped it into skri. Tira took the nuts from the oven with a pair of wooden tongs. "Let them cool, then try one."

Fern blew on the nuts until she could handle them. Then she cracked them and separated out the nutmeats. Roasting definitely improved the flavor. Fern couldn't decide whether they tasted more like peanuts or pecans.

"Our morning work's done now," Tira said. "We're free to do whatever we want."

Children were playing games on the sameg and adults were socializing. Fern wanted to be alone. All the unfamiliarity exhausted her. Grabbing some leftover skri, she returned to her mother's hut. Over the past few days, this had become home. She lay down on Mama's cot and drew comfort from it. She dozed off and woke refreshed, but hungry.

When she returned to the house, the family was already eating. Doran and Rina were there, too. Fern wondered about them. They acted like they were part of the household, and there were four pallets in the main room. They were cousins, but why didn't they have their own house? Maybe they were visiting. Customs here were so different. Fern hoped she could sort things out before she made too many blunders.

After lunch, she went back to her mother's hut. All those new experiences! She wished she had paper and pencil so she could write about them. After another nap, she bathed in the creek, clothes and all, washing her tunic as well as her body. She patted her hair. The tight plaits held together well and were quite practical. She didn't need to comb her hair several times a day and, being up off her neck, it was cooler in the heat of the afternoon. She walked through the woods to dry off.

Fern admired the size of the trees and thought, this is what a virgin forest looks like. She closed her eyes and sensed the immense power of the wilderness, yet she sensed no threat. She felt safe, at home, even welcome.

She followed the creek to the river, and the river to the lake. At the edge of the cliff she gazed at the waterfall with delight. A tree below her suddenly burst into a cloud of white. A puff of wind blew the cloud her way, a mass of airborne seeds like a dandelion's. She watched the little parachutes float up the surrounding hills and disperse in a thousand directions. Down near the woods, a well-worn path led to the pool at the foot of the cascade. Fern sat on a large rock. Tumbling water splashed into mist. Sunlight shone through the droplets, creating rainbows that came and went with the play of the sun and water and wind.

Fern knew there were places like this on Earth. Her family had vacationed in the Appalachian Mountains, but this place looked more like pictures of Hawaii. Her parents' promise to take them out West someday would never be fulfilled. Sadness clouded her enjoyment. How she missed her home planet!

On her way back through the meadow, she saw Doran sitting by the miaven tree on her mother's grave as though studying it. She didn't disturb him.

When Fern returned to the sameg, Andli motioned her over. She pinched the fabric on Fern's tunic in several places. Then she took the spare tunic from Fern's basket and handed it to her. Although Fern didn't understand the words, from Andli's gestures she gleaned that Andli wanted her to change clothes. The other tunic was threadbare, faded blue in color, but it fit slightly better than the yellow one. She gave the baggy tunic to Andli.

Returning to her seat in front of the house, Andli set aside her loom, turned the yellow tunic inside out, and began to stitch. *She must be taking it in for me.* Fern stayed to watch. "May I look at your loom?" she asked.

Andli smiled and nodded. Fern carefully lifted the loom and fingered the threads. They were soft but strong. She wanted to ask questions about the loom, but no one was present to translate. She thought it ingenious that, instead of weaving a flat, square cloth to be cut to fit and sewn together, Andli wove the garment in one piece.

When Fern set the loom down, Andli handed her a spindle and a ball of coarse yarn. She showed her how to hold the spindle and twist and stretch the yarn to make a finer thread. After a few awkward tries, Fern caught on. Her work was uneven, too thin in some places, too bulky in others, but whenever she looked up, Andli smiled with encouragement. Andli sang softly while she worked. Fern picked up the melody and hummed along.

By the time they finished, Fern's fingers were tired and had begun to blister. When Doran returned, Andli spoke to him. He gave Fern a little wooden box of ointment and instructed her to rub it on her hands. Almost immediately, the blisters shrank and the pain subsided. Fern put the ointment in her basket so she could use it later.

That evening on the sameg, the usual singing and dancing resumed. Fern thought back to the evening she and her mother sat here together and enjoyed the entertainment. It had been only two days ago but it seemed like eternity. So much had changed. Although she'd lost everyone and everything else, that evening she still had a mother who loved her. Now what did she have? She looked around at the crowd. A new family had taken her into their home, given her clothing and food, and treated her kindly, but was that enough? Inside, she felt like a hollow log.

One song ended and another began. As though acting on their own, Fern's feet began to jiggle to the music. Jorsil and Tira approached. "He'd like to dance with you. Would you like me to show you how?"

Fern wavered between a desire to dance and a dread of making a fool of herself. "Not right now. I'll just watch."

Jorsil left but Tira sat down beside Fern. With each new song or dance, she explained what it was about. When a woman told a story, Tira translated.

How long did Tira say the days were—the equivalent of twenty seven hours? When parents began to carry sleeping children to bed, Fern followed. This had been the longest day of her life. She paused at the doorway of the house to let her eyes adjust to the dimness. The fire across the sameg gave just enough light for her to see Doran asleep on a pallet in the main room. Why didn't the adults have private bedrooms? A blanket covered all but his shoulders, which were bare. Was she the only one who slept in clothes?

Fern tiptoed to the girls' room. As she parted the curtain, the rough fabric scratched the blisters on her palm. That reminded her to apply Doran's ointment before she slipped into bed. At least they used blankets because the nights were cool. How could she ever get used to these people and their strange ways? She was too tired to cry. The soft bedding caressed her skin and the herbal scent of the mattress soothed her to sleep.

CHAPTER 11
WAYS OF LIFE

In the morning, Fern successfully avoided embarrassment by looking away when adults were naked and waiting to use the latrine when no men were present. After breakfast, when she reached for her comb, she found the little box of ointment in her basket and looked at her hands. The blisters had healed overnight. Only a few red spots remained. "Amazing," she thought. She recalled what her mother had said about these people's medical skills. She showed Doran her palms and said, "Thank you."

While Andli and Rina fixed her hair, Fern watched Tira comb and plait Ara's. With her little finger, Tira parted Ara's hair in several places and braided each section, tying them off with bits of thread, singing softly or talking while she worked. Ara was the youngest in the family and the cutest. Dimples brightened her face when she smiled. Although Fern couldn't understand their words, Ara's smile warmed her heart. At the same time, she missed her own sisters terribly.

Tira wound the braids around Ara's head and secured them with wooden hair fasteners. Then she looked at Fern and said, "You'll learn to do this, also." Tira waited until Fern's hair was finished and said, "Let's go haul water. You can do this on your own after today. It doesn't matter when you do it, but I like to get mine over with in the morning."

As they emptied their water jugs into the cistern, Fern glanced at the house. The adults were lined up behind one another, fixing hair. Rina braided Taran's, and he worked on Doran's, who put the finishing touches on Andli's. "What a curious custom," she thought. She expected a big man like Taran to be clumsy at such delicate handwork, but his fingers slipped skillfully through Doran's hair, fashioning it into a pattern similar to what he'd worn the day before.

Tira handed her a basket. "We're going to collect nuts today." She gathered several children, handed out baskets, and tied a bag to her belt.

"What's that for?" Fern asked.

"For lenitrus, and other things."

Doran joined them and led them in a different direction this time. Again, they sang as they walked. Doran halted by a tree and gazed into its branches. Was he looking for nuts? Fern studied the tree. It had broad, oval leaves, but the stem of each leaf was attached to the middle of the oval, not the end. Several green balls hung from the branches. She'd come across other trees like this in the forest, but hadn't noticed any nuts.

"How do we get them down?" Fern asked.

"Wait for them to fall."

Doran lowered his eyes for a minute. Fern expected him to shake the tree, but when he spoke, the children fell to their hands and knees and searched for nuts among the leaf litter. Fern had gathered only a handful before she found one that had started to sprout.

"Let me have that," Tira said quickly and took it to Doran.

"Was that one bad?"

"Oh, no, they're good to eat when they sprout. Delicious. Sometimes we sprout them just to eat raw, but if we find one already sprouting, we plant it."

Doran took the sprout some distance from any other nut trees and, almost reverently, laid it on the ground and covered it with leaves.

Tira filled her basket, then helped the smaller children with theirs. Fern was the last to finish. Everyone faced the tree for a moment's silence. "We're thanking the tree for the nuts," Tira whispered.

On the way back, Doran lagged behind to gather leaves and place them in a bag at his waist. Tira also began harvesting lenitrus. "Whenever we go into the forest to gather firewood or nuts, or just take a walk, we do this, so what grows close to the village won't get used up." Fern wondered why she hadn't been given a bag but didn't ask. Progress was slow because they paused to ask and thank each plant. Fern grew impatient. The younger children, who were not gathering lenitrus, returned to the village ahead of them.

"Why did we thank the nut tree?" Fern asked. "We didn't pick the nuts from the tree."

"We thank all plants that give us food, or clothes, or other things. Doran asked the tree for permission to take its fallen nuts before we started to harvest them. That's why he planted your sprout. The nuts are the tree's way of having children, but it has more nuts than it needs for that, so it lets us take some, as long as we let its kind reproduce. Of course, we want them to reproduce, because we need them for food. But plants have a life force, the same as animals do, and we respect that."

"Yes, but plants can't really think, can they?"

"Not quite like we do, but…" she paused as though searching for the right words. "I can't explain it very well in English. Taran could. But it's like, everything is a part of God, even the plants and the water, even the rocks, so we try to be kind to everything and hope they'll be kind to us. We thank the river when we draw water. Even when we take stone from the mountains, we ask first and thank the mountain afterward."

Fern was quiet for a moment. Tira hadn't told her to thank the river. She'd seen people pause before they drew water, but she thought they were looking for something in the current. She hoped no one noticed her blunder. But how important was it, really? "Do you all believe that things have spirits? And you have to appease them?"

Tira stifled a laugh. "Not spirits like you're thinking about. Not like that, but everything has a soul, like people do. We don't need to appease them, but everything should be respected and treated the way we'd want to be treated if we were in its place."

Fern admitted this made sense, and it didn't conflict with anything her parents had taught.

As they approached the village, Fern noticed children climbing trees. "Do the trees mind if we climb them?"

"It's okay as long as we don't break anything. They like to play with us, especially the younger children. It's always a good idea to ask first, though."

Fern made note of this. She'd always liked climbing trees. "But how would I know the tree's answer?"

"If your mind is quiet, and you are in tune with the tree, you'll know."

Fern's thoughts drifted to the large live oak by her bedroom window back home. The first time her mother saw her in that tree, she'd said, "Aren't you getting too old for that?" Her father retorted, "I recall a young lady I dated once, a college student. She dared me to climb a tree in her parents' back yard, and she made it to the top while I was still trying to get to the first limb." Her mother punched him in the shoulder and said, "Don't go telling tales!"

Fern remembered sitting among the branches of that oak, feeling very much at home, as though the tree were a good friend. Now the tree was dead, a victim of the fire. Like her parents. She pressed her lips together to hold back tears.

By the time they returned to the sameg, Fern's legs ached. But Tira said, "Now all we have to do is get firewood."

Fern groaned inwardly. She didn't want to admit any weakness to Tira, but she needed to rest. "Can't we do that later?"

"Sure. Go ahead and rest. We'll do it this afternoon."

Fern's legs complained all the way to her mother's hut. She sat in her mother's chair and rocked until the cramping eased. The motion soothed her. So much to absorb—the unfamiliar way of life, the very foreign language. Life here was pleasant and the work not that hard, but she was so easily fatigued. It helped to have time alone with her thoughts. She was glad no one bothered her in the hut. It seemed understood that this was her private space, and her need for privacy was respected. She looked at the sky through a small hole in the roof where a storm must have disturbed the thatch. She should tell Taran about it. Instead, she fell asleep in the rocking chair.

Fern was hungry when she woke. People were gathering on the sameg, helping themselves to fresh skri. Fern ate one but it didn't satisfy her hunger.

She'd reached for another when Tira joined her. "Is it too early for lunch?" Fern asked.

"No." Tira ladled two bowls of soup and handed one to Fern. They walked over to the house where Andli was working on Fern's yellow tunic. Tala and Ara and a group of their friends were eating lenitrus. Fern carefully set her bowl down and adjusted her tunic as she seated herself. Before she started to eat, Tira looked silently at her food for a minute as though saying "grace." Fern followed suit.

"Have some salad," Tira said. She examined the leaves and said, "You can eat all of these."

Fern decided to try something different. She split her skri in half and tried to make a sandwich with the greens. The bread was crumbly, so she had to be careful to hold it together. The other children watched closely. One of the youngest, who apparently didn't understand that Fern didn't know their language, said something to her.

"She wants to know why you put lenitrus in your skri," Tira said, then answered the child in their language. "I told them you tried to make a sandwich, and that people eat that way on Earth." Tala attempted to make herself a sandwich. When she took a bite, it all fell apart into her lap. She laughed, as did the other children, and Fern couldn't help laughing with them.

After this, the children seemed to lose their initial bashfulness and started asking Fern questions. The older ones directed their inquiries to Tira. A dialog in their language followed. Tira spoke with an air of importance. Fern occasionally heard her name, and when the children glanced at her, she felt like the subject of gossip. Her discomfort finally drove her to ask, "What's going on?"

"They have questions about Earth and the people there."

"What are you telling them?"

"Lots of things."

When a girl asked another question, Fern demanded, "What did she say?"

Tira squirmed. "I told them about hamburgers and meat. She asked if meat makes your hair yellow." Before Fern could speak, she added hastily, "No one here has blonde hair."

Fern huffed. "Let me tell them. I know a lot more about Earth than you do."

Tira nodded and continued to translate.

To Fern's surprise, the children had no questions about the great accomplishments of mankind on Earth, but were curious about little things of everyday life. They were especially fascinated by animals. Fern became fatigued long before the children tired of questioning her. Finally, she asked Tira to tell them she would answer more later. One child approached Fern and hugged her before leaving, and several others did the same.

After they left, Tira confessed, "I was trying to show off at your expense. I'm sorry. I didn't mean to hurt your feelings."

"It's okay," Fern replied. She shifted position. Her legs were going numb.

Tira started picking up dirty dishes. When Fern stood up to help, it took a minute for her legs to work properly. There was so much to get used to here.

* * *

Fern planned to water the little miaven tree on her mother's grave after lunch, but the sky clouded over and thunder rumbled. She retired to her mother's hut for a nap and to wait out the storm. Later, when she returned to the sameg, she noticed that, while everywhere else was wet, the ground there was dry. "I wonder how that happens," she thought, but neither Taran nor Tira were around to ask.

Fern noticed Andli stirring something in a large clay pot at the fire pit and went over to look. It wasn't soup. Andli smiled and, with a large pair of wooden tongs, pulled out a piece of green cloth and took it to the river. Fern followed. Andli rinsed it, wrung out the water, and held it up. Fern recognized what had been her yellow tunic. The green dye covered the faded spots. Fern was pleased with the color. "Thank you," she said.

Tira handed Fern a sling for wood and a bag for lenitrus. "Let's go fetch firewood now. After you get to know the woods better, you can do it on your own."

"On my own? Aren't you afraid I'd get lost?"

"Why should you get lost? Even if you did, we'd find you."

Fern didn't tell Tira she had no such fear, but she wondered why they didn't worry about her. If someone did get lost, really lost, what hope would there be of finding them in this almost unlimited wilderness?

Tira attached her bag to her belt. Fern lamented, "I wish I had a belt."

"Oh! I'm sorry." Tira rushed into the house and brought out a short rope. "This should do for now."

Later, when they returned to the sameg, several chattering children met them. One little girl held out her hands and offered Fern a long, narrow strip with colorful beads worked into it. The child wore a similar one at her waist. Fern hesitated, unsure what was expected of her.

Tira smiled. "This is a gift for you. Her brother made it."

"Thank you." Fern tied the belt around her waist. "Which one is her brother?"

Tira pointed to a young man taking skri from an oven. It was Aldan, who had brought her a biscuit yesterday.

"How do I say thank you in your language?"

"Tekuyate."

Fern tried to repeat the word. The children tittered.

Tira broke it down into syllables. "Tay-koo-yah-tay."

Fern rose above her timidity, approached Aldan, and held up an end of the belt. "Tekuyate." He smiled. Fern blushed. He was so handsome, built like an athlete, with green eyes and a cleft chin.

The belt helped her tunic fit better, but it was still not as nice as Tira's. Fern was anxious to wear the refurbished green one.

Later that afternoon, Taran convened a handful of children and young people, including her and Tira, for a language class. Her fellow students were interested in learning English. "You can learn our language while you help me teach," he said. They made themselves comfortable under a large tree near the sameg.

Aldan was walking across the sameg. He glanced their way and came over. Taran asked him to join them. He sat across from Fern. Sheepishly, she checked her lap to be sure her tunic hid her nether parts. It seemed everyone, except the very young children, managed to somehow protect their modesty.

Taran spoke alternately in English and their language. The other pupils seemed to follow English fairly well, but Fern couldn't make heads or tails of what he was saying in the other tongue. At a pause in the lesson, she asked, "What do you call your language?" She expected a reply related to their ethnic group.

Instead, Taran uttered the most unpronounceable word she had yet to hear. Then he smiled at her puzzlement and said, "Human Talk." The lesson concluded with the understanding that in day-to-day life the students would point to objects and teach Fern their words, and she would do the same in English.

She lingered behind. "Why are your words so weird?"

"Do you mean, why are they so different from human languages on Earth?"

"Yes."

"Some of our words are human, but the basic language is not."

"Who made your language, if not humans?" She knew the answer before he spoke.

"It's the language of the thortles." Taran's face darkened. Fern had never before seen him angry. He sighed and sat on the ground. Fern joined him.

"We speak their language only because our people were robbed of our own. They captured our ancestors one by one, from different lands and civilizations, over hundreds, maybe thousands of years. We lost our native cultures and languages and couldn't talk to one another except in the thortle language. Actually, what we speak is a pidgin that accommodates our physical abilities and human experiences. The thortles can make sounds no human can, and of course humans can make sounds thortles can't."

"Why?"

"Because the mouth parts are different." He took a deep breath. "Thortles don't have lungs, like we do. They make their noises with various parts of their bodies, as well as their mouths."

"How?"

"Like a grasshopper or cicada."

Tira's description of a thortle as a cockroach as big as she came to mind. She shuddered.

Taran continued. "Many of the sounds we use are imitations of theirs, but not identical to them. Of course, our language has been enriched to include words for things such as emotions, which thortles don't possess, and to describe things on this world that we had no thortle words for. We also have vocabulary that was probably borrowed from our ancestors' original languages, and a few words visitors have brought back from Earth. I believe our word for love, 'aloa,' came from the Hawaiian aloha. The thortles have no word for love. I've found other connections between some of our words and their equivalent in Earth languages. 'Salut' probably came from Spanish, and 'mi manchi,' 'I miss you,' is Italian. Thortles have no use for such niceties."

"The word 'nuts' is English?"

Taran nodded. "Our ancestor Moses gave us that word."

"Moses?"

"He and his mate Rila are whom we call our First Parents. We are all descended from them. Six generations ago, over one hundred years in Earth time, their three children and their families, and about a dozen others, came here. Since then, a handful more have joined us by wrashiru, but we are all descended from the few who originally arrived." He stood. "I think this is enough for today."

CHAPTER 12
MARRIAGE CUSTOMS

That evening on the sameg, Aldan approached Fern and held out his hand.

"He wants you to dance with him," Tira said.

Fern lowered her eyes. "Tell him I don't know how."

"You can learn. I'll help you." She pulled Fern up with her. The three of them held hands and Tira said, "Follow our lead."

Fern focused on her feet and tried to imitate their movements, but her legs tangled and she tripped. Aldan caught her and set her back on her feet. His arms were strong and steady. She covered her uneasiness with a laugh. Aldan laughed, too.

Tira called to the musicians. "I asked them to slow the tempo," she said.

Now Fern could follow their lead better, but her legs quickly tired and she was relieved when the dance was over. She thanked Aldan and told Tira that was enough for the night.

The next dance was accompanied by drumming. Rina energetically pounded on her cloth-covered stump. Fern moved to her side for a closer look. It was a drum made from a hollow section of tree trunk, with two stubs of branches still attached. A tough fabric was stretched over both ends for drum heads. Carvings of dancers, stars, and moons circled the sides. Once the dance had ended, Rina showed Fern how she played the sides and stubs as well as the heads. Each part of the instrument made a different sound. Jorsil, who had been dancing, joined them. A song was next. Jorsil played a wooden flute and the village sang. Fern picked up the melody and hummed along.

During the night, Fern had to use the latrine and was glad for a moon to light her way. Several people slept on the sameg, mostly older adolescents and young adults. She recognized Jorsil as one of them. The boys and girls, for the most part, slept separately, but she did see one couple entwined in each other's arms. She thought about Aldan and wondered about courtship and dating among her new people.

* * *

The following day began much like the previous ones. When the village gathered on the sameg before sunrise, Taran attempted to teach Fern the morning song. She stumbled over the pronunciation so badly she decided to just listen while everyone else sang.

Her now-green tunic was dry. Andli stitched a row of wooden beads around the neckline and gave it to Fern. With her new belt, it fit better. Fern no longer felt shabby.

After chores, she retreated to her mother's hut as usual. She lay on her mother's cot and let her mind wander beyond the hut. How far from the village had she ventured? Not more than a few miles. Fern had noticed people drifting into the forest alone or in pairs, not to return for half a day. Is that what Taran did? Children could be found playing alone in quiet places, sometimes with their dolls, or sitting silently in trees. That vast wilderness called to her. She almost understood why the elders went "walking." She fell asleep.

An approaching thunderstorm disturbed her rest. She remembered the hole in the roof. It had grown larger, but she was in no mood to return to the village. A little rain wouldn't hurt. During the ensuing downpour, she automatically prepared to move to a drier spot, but no rain came through the roof. What kept it from leaking? She fell back to sleep and by the time she returned to the sameg for lunch, the question had left her mind.

The lunch menu included sprouted nuts, and someone had prepared a "salad dressing" to accompany them. They were sweet and succulent. Fern downed several before Taran admonished, "Go easy or you'll get a belly ache."

Later that day, she went into the forest by herself for firewood. She heard voices and followed the sounds. Through a screen of leaves, she glimpsed Andli and Doran sitting in a cozy little bower, talking and laughing. Andli must have sensed her presence. She stood up and faced Fern. She was naked! She and Fern locked eyes.

Fern threw down her firewood and ran back to her mother's hut. How could Andli do such a thing? Fern felt betrayed, just as if she'd found her own mother in another man's embrace. She rocked in her mother's chair, trying to banish the awful scene from her mind. Another storm blew in. Fern stayed in the chair, rocking furiously, glad of the thunder and lightning, too confused to cry. The storm moved on, but Fern didn't go back to the village. She wished she never had to. Where else could she go? More than ever, she wanted to go home. Finally, she let herself cry, wiping her face on her tunic. She grew hungry, but she didn't care.

Taran came to the doorway. "Fern?"

"What do you want."

"May I come in?"

She tried to ignore him, hoping he'd leave. Instead, he came in and sat on her mother's cot, facing her.

"I believe I know what's troubling you."

She certainly wasn't about to tell him what she'd seen!

But he said, "You saw Andli and Doran in the forest together."

He knew! She looked at him like he was a crazy man.

"You know we do things differently here. We have plural marriages." He paused to let this sink in. "Andli and I, and Rina and Doran, are married together. Such arrangements have been a necessity for us as far back as our memory goes."

Fern gave him a skeptical look.

"You see, before our people came here, when we were slaves of the thortles, they would often separate families and send people away to work elsewhere. When a couple was separated, each might take a new mate. If the old mate returned, that person would then have two mates. Sometimes three or more people would marry together and the children would be shared, so they would still have a family if a parent was taken away. After we came here, we continued the practice of taking more than one mate."

Fern scowled.

"There's another, more important, reason. There are so few of us, we have to be careful not to interbreed. Only certain unions are permitted to produce children, but sometimes we fall in love with someone we shouldn't have children with. When we were young, Rina and I fell in love, but we're too closely related to have children together. So Rina married Doran, and they had three children, Jorsil, Donal, and Tala."

Fern looked at him in surprise. "I thought all the children belonged to you and Andli."

"They do. They belong to all four of us. You remember Lila, whom you met when you first came here. She and I mated first, and together we have a son. Unfortunately Lila wasn't happy living in the mountains. I love the mountains, and wasn't happy living by the sea, so we agreed to part. She took on a new mate, but we still love each other.

"Andli and Doran love each other, too, but they're too closely related to have children. Andli married someone else and had a son. He's now grown and lives in the village by the sea. Unfortunately, her husband died. After this, I married Andli, and Tira and Ara are our children. The four of us share a household and rear our children together. I love Andli. She's my wife. I love Rina, too. She's also my wife. And I love Doran, our husband. We are all married together. Does this make sense?"

Reluctantly, Fern nodded. It did make sense. She knew some cultures on Earth allowed men to have more than one wife, but she had never heard of anything quite like this.

"As for you, when you are ready to marry, you'll have your choice of any man on this planet, since none are closely related to you."

Fern blushed. She didn't want to think about marriage right now. How could she share a husband with another woman? Or have two husbands herself? She shook her head.

Taran put an arm around her and led her back to their house. Andli, Doran, and Rina waited in the main room but the children were, thankfully, absent. Fern didn't know what to do. She could barely look at Andli, and she wouldn't look at Doran at all. Rina stepped forward and put an arm around Taran. She said something he translated as, "This is the love of my life." They smiled into each other's eyes and Fern felt the warmth between them. Rina then put an arm around Doran and said, through Taran, "This is my mate, the father of my children." Doran smiled into Rina's eyes with no less warmth. Finally, she hugged Andli and spoke. Taran said, "The literal English translation would be, 'This is my closer-than-sister. She is also mother of my children.'" Both women then hugged Fern, and Taran translated, "You are our daughter. We love you as much as we love our other children and as much as we love one another."

Fern detected no jealousy or competition. It was true. The four of them were as one. Still, she hung her head. How could she be expected to live like this?

Doran didn't attempt to hug her, only took both of her hands and held them. A wave of trust flowed up her arms and through her. She raised her eyes to him and, with a sob, threw her arms around him. Doran patted her back, much as her father used to.

Taran spoke again, "You are our daughter, but don't worry, we won't try to take the place of your parents. You remain their child as well. Think of yourself as having three mothers and three fathers instead of only one of each."

Fern almost choked on her tears. "I know. My mother gave me to you and Andli before she died. But I don't think she understood it was the four of you."

Taran smiled sadly. "No, we hid nothing from her, but we didn't burden her with that information. We would have told her if she'd asked. I believe she had some idea of our arrangement, but she had so much else on her mind."

"But why didn't you tell me?"

"Estut miryit. I'm sorry. We planned to give you time to get used to us first. We didn't intend to have you find out this way."

Fern melted with exhaustion. Andli put her on her own bed and gently rubbed her back. The others withdrew. Doran returned with some tea. Fern sat up to drink it. The tea both strengthened her and helped her relax.

That night, Fern went to bed early but couldn't sleep. She thought about people falling in love with someone they couldn't marry. Everyone here had looked so happy. Who could have guessed their relationships suffered the same troubles as people's on Earth? Andli had been widowed, and Taran divorced. Fern thought about Lila. She and Taran had gone to Earth as a couple, taking Tira with them. She tried not to think about that.

When Tira came in, Fern asked, "Isn't it weird for your mother to have two husbands? And your father to have two wives?"

"Not for me. I grew up this way."

"So Tala isn't really your sister. And Jorsil and Donal aren't really your brothers. They're really cousins."

"Biologically, they're cousins, but they really *are* my sister and brothers, the same way Ara is. And Rina and Doran are really my parents, the same as Andli and Taran. I also have two other brothers, Tiril and Rufan. They both live in the village by the sea. Tiril is staying with his mother, Lila, and Rufan is married. You'll meet them some day."

Fern was silent for a minute. "Since Jorsil and Donal are not biologically your brothers, would you be allowed to marry one of them?"

"No, we're still too closely related."

"I guess it would be too weird, anyway, like a step-sister and step-brother where I come from getting married."

Tira made no reply.

"I really like Taran and Andli, and it hasn't been hard to think of them as my foster parents, but I've been thinking of Rina and Doran as more like an aunt and uncle."

"That's okay. They understand. No one is forcing you to feel affection for anyone."

"How do you know they understand?"

A faint rustling sound told her Tira was shrugging her shoulders. "We just know these things about one another."

CHAPTER 13
THE WEKA

Fern got tired of asking Taran, and especially Tira, about every little thing. Instead, she quietly observed the goings-on in the village and tried to figure things out on the own. Sometimes, however, she had to ask. One day, a young woman was nursing a baby Fern thought belonged to another. She asked Tira.

"Yes. They do this a lot, especially if the women are mates in the same household."

Another time she asked Taran, "I've noticed that most couples seem to have three children."

"You are correct. Every woman is expected to bear three children. That way our numbers increase. We don't have more because we need to be able to feed everyone, but there are many waiting to be born here, so we need to multiply, but slowly."

Although most households had children, only adults lived in the house next door. Three of them were Tira's grandparents. Tira tried to teach Fern the Human Talk word for grandparent, but it included sounds completely foreign to her. Grandparents were teachers, leading groups of children into the forest and instructing them in crafts. The great-grandparents primarily talked to children and told stories. The word for that generation was also unpronounceable to Fern, but she was able to master the word for the generation of great-great-grandparents, the weka.

For Fern, an aura of mystery surrounded the weka. She seldom saw them carry firewood or water. They dabbled in other occupations only at whim.

Much of the time they sat under their awnings, silently, eyes closed. How old were these people in Earth reckoning? Fern asked Tira. Although she couldn't give her a figure, Tira said, "We frequently live past one hundred in Earth years."

Her faith in Andli now restored, Fern took comfort in sitting with her and learning to spin. Andli had nearly completed the tunic she was weaving. Fern watched her carefully remove it from the loom, curious to see how she finished it.

That afternoon, a man carrying a basket of thread came over. He faced Fern, put a hand to his chest, and said, "Olan." When it dawned on her he had introduced himself, she did the same. He sat down, looked at the yarn Fern had spun, and nodded with approval. Andli smiled at Olan and handed him her empty loom. After closing his eyes for a moment in what appeared to be silent prayer, he began to string the loom with red thread. He and Andli sang while they worked. Fern hummed.

She studied Olan's face. His eyes were the same color as Andli's, and the two seemed quite fond of each other. She didn't think Andli had a third husband. Could he be her brother?

An especially pretty young woman, who introduced herself as Hansa, joined them. Fern began to feel uncomfortable. Everyone knew her better than she knew them. Hansa was making a hat. Andli handed her pieces of leftover thread which Hansa worked into the hat.

Later, Fern asked Tira about Olan.

"Yes, he's Andli's brother."

"I was surprised to see him weaving."

"Why?"

"I guess I thought of it as women's work."

"We don't have 'women's work' or 'men's work.' Everybody learns as many skills as possible. Then they can choose what they like to do. Everything has to get done, of course."

The next morning, Taran sat under the awning next door and beckoned Fern to join him. "It's about time you became acquainted with the extended family. These are my parents, Atla and Hatir."

"Salut," Fern said.

The couple nodded.

"And this is Andli's mother, Noba. From time to time you'll accompany them to gather food and other things, and assist them with food preparation. They'll also teach you other skills."

Fern nodded. The grandparents rose and went about their business. The three weka who also lived in the house emerged and sat in their places.

Fern remembered having to visit her Irish great-grandfather in the nursing home. Her parents always made a point of spending at least an hour with him, but all he did was sleep. It was so boring. One time, Fern complained and was chastised when they got home. Afterward, she struggled to appear respectful, but in her mind, sleep was the main occupation of the very old.

"This is Dorsa and Geltan. They are my and Rina's great-grandparents. And this is Nasi. She's Andli and Doran's great-grandmother."

Fern met their eyes. They were very unlike her great-grandfather. Their eyes were bright and keen. One by one, they held her gaze. Fern felt naked, as if she had no secrets from them.

Geltan spoke. Taran nodded and replied in their language. Then Dorsa looked at Fern and said something. Taran smiled and interpreted, "She says you have nothing to fear from them."

Nothing to fear from them? What could that mean? Fern almost shuddered. Were they able to read her mind? After the visit, she asked Taran, "What did Geltan say about me?"

"He said you are troubled and unhappy. He thinks your road to healing will be long and difficult."

Fern frowned. How could anyone expect her to be happy and untroubled after all she'd been through! She didn't voice this to Taran. Instead, she grumbled, "Don't they get tired of sitting around all the time with nothing to do?" At least her old granddad could watch TV.

Taran smiled. "Don't be fooled by appearances. They have plenty to do."

"Like what? They're too old to do much."

"Don't let your notions of old age cloud your mind. The weka do more than you realize."

"Like what?"

"I'll explain another time."

"But where are your grandparents?"

"Gota and Korsim live in the village by the sea. Bregan lives in that house." He pointed across the sameg. "And Picto is walking."

Again, there was that allusion to the curious practice of elderly people walking about the wilderness. "By herself?"

"No, she's accompanied by Handir."

They'd reached the center of the sameg. Taran pointed to the fire pit. "Noba is ready to show you how to make skri." He made no indication of accompanying her.

"Aren't you going to translate?"

He shook his head. "All you need to do is pay attention and do what she shows you."

* * *

One afternoon, Fern heard raised voices and noticed two children at the tetherball court squabbling. Geltan immediately went to the children and gently laid his hands on their shoulders. Fern watched to see what happened next. Geltan and the children talked in low voices, then the children hugged and resumed playing.

Upon reflection, Fern realized this was the only quarrel she'd seen since she'd been here. People joked with one another, but she'd observed no cross words, no aggression, nor any unfriendly teasing.

At times, Fern couldn't help becoming sullen or cross. Only her innate shyness saved her from making a public spectacle of herself. When she felt like lashing out, she would escape to her mother's hut until her mood improved. Even if she were in the middle of work, no one tried to stop her.

After one such episode, she apologized to Taran.

"Everyone understands you've been through much trauma," he said. "And no one thinks badly of you. You do the right thing when you go to your hut at such times."

"I don't see anyone else acting this way. Why am I the only one?"

"Because you grew up differently, in a culture where competition and conflict are the norm. Our children are taught from birth how to relate to one another peacefully."

"My parents tried to raise me that way."

He nodded. "There's a genetic reason as well." Taran paused and seemed to struggle for composure. "The thortles tried to breed aggressive tendencies out of us. They wanted compliant slaves, easy to manage. On the surface, that may appear to be a good thing, but I wonder if it resulted in some weaknesses in us." He smiled. "We welcome your fresh genes. You may add some things we lack."

"Even with my bad temper?"

"You manage your temper well. And it will become easier for you in time."

* * *

That night, Fern woke to the sound of rain on the roof and wondered about the young people sleeping on the sameg. She expected Jorsil to come inside, but if he did, she didn't hear him. In the morning, although the forest was damp from rain, the ground within the circle of huts was dry. How? She asked Tira.

"We put an umbrella over the sameg," she said.

"Umbrella?"

Tira laughed. "Not a physical umbrella, but that's the closest English word I could think of. It's done mentally. Maybe 'force field' would be a better term." Tira tried to explain how it was done, but Fern had no idea what she was talking about, so Tira said, "Taran can explain it better than I can."

When Taran joined them for breakfast, she asked him.

"Some of us have an ability to put up a protective shield. It's not a material shield, and it's not strong, but it can divert rain and wind, and keep in warmth. We can also put one around a person to protect him from minor injuries." He didn't try to explain the "mechanics" of the process as Tira had. "This is not routinely done. If one so gifted is caught in the rain, he allows himself to get wet. But to have our sameg turn to mud after every shower would be quite uncomfortable, so the weka shield it. One must be in a deep meditative state to do that. They've extended this comfort to you when you are in your hut because it was hastily thatched. We'd planned for it to be a temporary shelter only, so we put little effort into its construction."

When she saw the weka next door sitting under their awning, Fern went over to thank them. Even though she spoke English, they seemed to understand her meaning and nodded in acknowledgement.

* * *

Besides her family, what Fern missed most was reading. She used to read herself to sleep at night, but here she saw no books or anything that looked like written language. Nor had she seen anyone staring purposely at an object as though reading. Tira had told her Taran would teach her how to read. After language class one day, she asked him.

"It's true, we have no books as you know them, but we have the libraries of the universe at our disposal."

"What? How do you—do you go to other planets to read?"

"No, we project our minds, much as you did when you visited your sisters. Of course, it helps to know the language. We can read writings from the thortle world, but we must take care not to be detected. We are slowly amassing our own library with works we've translated from other languages, and ones we ourselves have written. Since I can read English, I've translated some books."

"But—where is this library?"

"No *place*. It's a mental structure. As you learn our language, I'll teach you to read it. In the meantime, you can access books in English. You have the ability to do this, but you'll need training."

The first step in training was learning to meditate.

Taran sat with Fern in her mother's hut. First, he taught her to breathe with her diaphragm. Once she was comfortable with this, he said, "As you breathe in, let your mind expand with your lungs. Then open your consciousness as you breathe out. Between breaths, rest and experience oneness."

Although she tried to concentrate, her mind wandered. Little thoughts flittered here and there, interfering with her focus. After the session, Fern told Taran about this problem.

"That's normal. Don't let it disturb you. When you catch those thoughts, acknowledge them, set them aside, and return to your purpose."

The next time she was alone in her mother's hut, Fern tried to meditate as Taran had taught her. Her mind wandered to her family. She remembered how she used to share a room with her sisters and how they would get into her things. After they moved into their house, it had been so nice to finally have her own space. Now she shared a room with new sisters who left her few belongings alone, but she missed her own sisters and would trade anything to be with them again, even share a room.

She sat in her mother's chair, feeling her closeness, and felt herself reach out to her sisters. Suddenly, she found herself in a classroom on Earth. Her youngest sister sat at a desk, doodling, paying no attention to the teacher. Then she laid her head on the desk and began to cry. Fern wanted to go to her. The teacher took the child's hand and led her from the room. Fern followed them down the hall to a door labeled "Guidance." Fern couldn't hear what anyone said, but a pretty lady handed her sister a box of tissues and held her hand.

Fern put her arms around her. "It's okay," she whispered. "Mama and Daddy are in Heaven, but they still love you. I'm alive, but far, far away and I can't come back, but I still love you." Fern felt her sister relax. Soon her tears ceased. The lady spoke to the child, who nodded and returned to the classroom. To the counselor, Fern said, "Thank you."

Instantly, Fern was at her grandparents' house. Grandpa slept in his chair with a newspaper on his lap. She found Grandma on her bed napping. Fern hugged her and said, "I'm okay, don't worry about me. Thank you for taking care of the little ones." Then she returned to the living room and told her grandfather the same.

She came to herself back in the hut. Her heart felt lighter. Had she dreamed? It had felt so real.

Later, she spoke to Taran about it. He nodded. "It was a real experience. An etheric projection—ethenos. You are progressing well with meditation. You're beginning to reach out. Soon you'll be able to contact others through your mind, and you'll discover new abilities you don't know you possess. You'll also have better control over your powers. Don't force yourself. Let it flow." He went on, "Continue to contact your relatives. You've found a safe way to visit them, but be cautious about contact with anyone you're not familiar with."

Contact anyone else? That hadn't crossed Fern's mind. "Who shouldn't I contact? Would somebody try to contact me? Why? What could happen?"

"We have to be careful not to give the thortles a clue to our existence."

Fern was taken aback. "But, do you think I could accidentally contact them?"

"You wouldn't contact the thortles themselves, because they have no psychic powers. But some of our distant cousins on the thortle world go 'fishing' for people with psychic ability. I wouldn't want them to find you."

Fern winced and looked at the sky.

Taran smiled. "I didn't mean to alarm you. I think if any contact was made, you'd instinctively withdraw. But stay alert."

"How would I know it was them?"

"You would know it wasn't one of us. Have you ever had a bad feeling about someone and didn't know why?"

She nodded.

"It would be the same, maybe stronger. You'd have a sense that something wasn't right. As long as you pay attention to those feelings, you'll be safe. We look out for one another here, and we look out for you. That's another thing the weka do. We'd warn you if we were aware of any threat."

Fern had felt safe. Was that only an illusion? She closed her eyes and reached out with her mind. She detected nothing troubling. Yes, she was safe.

CHAPTER 14
FEAST OF THE FULL MOONS

The days settled into a routine: meals, chores, language class, instructions by adults on various skills, evening gatherings on the sameg. Fern spent her spare time in her mother's hut, practicing meditation and trying to visit her sisters by ethenos. When successful, she found their lives playing out as well as could be expected for two orphans in the arms of their grandparents. Whether warmed by these visions or disappointed when she failed at ethenos, she allowed herself a good cry afterward.

Every day, Fern visited her mother's grave. The ground cover had taken hold, and only the mound showed where the soil had been disturbed. By now she could detect other slight mounds indicating previous burials. She counted eight and there might be more, older ones.

The small miaven tree flourished and put on new growth. Fern found other miavens in the forest, small trees with no practical value she could discover, but pretty, with leaves drooping gracefully from their branches. Since they grew in shady, damp places, she kept hers well-watered. More than once, she'd seen Doran sitting by the tree as though in meditation.

Fern watched the villagers play games and sports, wishing she could join them. By their gestures and the friendly tone of their words, she knew she was invited but, by merely observing, she couldn't figure out the rules and didn't want to ask Tira or bother Taran.

One day she watched a footrace and the next time the runners lined up, she joined them. She got off to a fast start, feeling the exhilaration of blood pumping through her muscles, her bare feet grasping the ground, pulling her ahead of the pack. Then an older girl, Tirna, passed her, looked back, and shouted. What was she yelling about? Fern took it as an insult and, stung to the quick, stopped running. She stepped out of the way of the other runners, her limbs trembling with disappointment.

Tira followed her. "Why did you stop running?"

"She yelled at me."

"She was only encouraging you. She said to run faster and catch up with her."

Fern frowned. "Why would she say that?"

Tira put her hands on her hips. "The point of a race is for everyone to get better, not necessarily to come in first."

Fern tried to hide her tears. She retreated to her mother's hut. These people were so hard to understand. She just didn't fit in. After this, she avoided games entirely. Going after firewood was enough exercise.

* * *

Her loom restrung with red thread, Andli spent much of her time weaving. Tira said, "She's making you a new tunic."

Fern was pleased. The color would look good on her. Andli gave Fern a basket of red fiber to spin into thread. The hours spent with Andli each day while she worked on the new tunic comforted Fern almost as much as visiting her sisters.

One day, Andli took Tira and Fern and a handful of children to a marshy area. She paused before a large clump of reeds and Fern knew she was asking permission to pick them. "This is what we make cloth from," Tira said and translated Andli's instructions. "Look for stalks that have finished going to seed and break them off near the roots, just don't pull them up." They gathered armloads of stalks and carried them to the village. Andli placed them in a large clay crock filled with water, took a handful of mud from the river, and dropped it into the crock.

"Something like fungi in the mud will help the soft parts decompose," Tira explained. "Then the fibers are easier to extract."

Within a few days, the crock was full of slime. They removed the fibers, rinsed them, and laid them in the sun to dry. When Tira and Fern returned later to turn the fibers over, the crock was gone. "Where is it?" Fern asked.

"Andli took it back to the marsh and dumped it."

"By herself?"

Tira nodded.

Fern found the empty crock by the fire pit and tried to lift it. Even empty it was heavy. She had no idea Andli was so strong.

The next day, Andli led the group into the woods. "We're going to gather the ingredients for dye," Tira said. They collected seeds, roots, and leaves from various plants. Andli explained everything, including the chemistry involved, and Tira translated, but it was too much for Fern to absorb. When Andli came to a plant called tolit, she allowed no one else to touch it and spent more time than usual communing with it. Finally, she snapped the stem off above the root. A milky substance oozed out. Andli collected this in a small bowl, squeezing the stem to get all she could. Then she laid the remains on the ground where the plant had grown, harvested seeds from a neighbor, and planted them, reverently, in the same place. Afterward, she spent another minute with her head bowed.

"She's thanking the plant for giving up its life," Tira whispered.

Fern nodded impatiently.

Tira went on, "The sap is the most important ingredient in dye. Andli spent so much time on this plant because its sacrifice was not to support life, but for human vanity."

"Oh."

The lesson wasn't over. Tira and Fern helped Andli sort their gleanings and crush and grind them into powders and pastes. They watched Andli weigh each constituent with her hands and add it to a pot of boiling water. The water turned deep green. While the dye cooked, Andli stirred in the dry fibers. Once they turned color, she removed them and draped them over a rack to dry.

The next day, Andli set all the children of the household to spinning. By now, Fern could make a smooth, strong thread. If a strand was not to

Andli's satisfaction, she would re-spin it. Smugly, Fern noted that Andli often re-spun Tira's thread but seldom found fault with hers.

Andli began working on Fern's new tunic to the exclusion of other tasks, as though she were in a hurry to finish. Rina even did her chores. While Fern helped Andli spin, Rina and Jorsil spent their time next door with the weka. Fern wondered if Rina and Andli had had a falling out. Did Rina resent having to do Andli's chores?

When the new tunic neared completion, Andli used the green thread to embroider borders around the neck, arms, and hem. As the pattern took shape, Fern recognized it—fern fronds! There was a plant with fern-like leaves called "ahnti." Apparently, Tira or Taran had told Andli what Fern's name meant and she used ahnti leaves as a model.

Fern felt excitement building in the village. New shelves were built near the fire pit for freshly woven baskets. Children gathered seed pods that resembled pine cones and extracted the seeds. When Andli no longer needed Fern's assistance, she sent her to help them.

It was arduous work. Fern struggled to pry open a pod and tore a fingernail. Narvil, a young man from language class, sat down beside her and said, "I show you." Fern cringed. Narvil always seemed impatient with her lack of progress in Human Talk.

Gently, he took the pod from her and, starting at the top, deftly pulled apart a few layers and shook out tiny seeds. Then he handed the pod back to Fern.

"Tekuyate." She wanted to ask Narvil why they went to so much trouble for so few seeds but couldn't find the words. She resorted to English. "What are they for?"

Narvil gave her a quizzical look.

Fern looked for Tira, but she was nowhere around. "Are they food?"

Narvil grinned and nodded. "Yes. Sweet."

Fern bit into a seed, but it was so bitter she made a face. Narvil laughed and stood up. "Come with me." She followed him to the fire pit. He sprinkled a few seeds on a hot rock, rotating them until they turned brown.

Then he popped a few in his mouth and gave Fern the rest. Delicious! Toasting made them sweet.

Cooks ground the seeds and used them to make cookies. After these were baked and cooled, they were stored in the baskets. Anyone caught stealing a taste was scolded. This didn't stop the children, and some adults, from trying. Jorsil managed to sneak a few cookies and gave one to Fern. She had missed sweets almost as much as meat. Her longing was temporarily satisfied.

Fern guessed the reason for the festive preparations when she noticed that both moons were approaching full at the same time. She asked Taran.

"Yes," he said. "This happens about every year and a half in Earth time. The large moon will grow full sixteen times and the small one twenty three times before they're full together. We feel compelled to celebrate. It's our main holiday, like your Christmas."

Narvil sent his sister to Fern with a necklace of colorful beads. Fern was puzzled. This was the second young man who had sent her a gift. She asked Tira, "Does this mean he likes me?"

Tira said, "Yes."

"Should I accept it?"

"Of course."

"But what does it mean? What does he want from me?"

"That you look on him kindly. It's not a marriage proposal, if that's what you're worried about."

Fern knew all the young men saw her as a potential mate because she wasn't related to them. But her fantasies of love and marriage centered around her old way of life on Earth, and she hadn't given up hope of going home. If she were to marry a boy here, she'd have to leave him if she returned. Then, what if she fell in love with someone on Earth? She'd face the same quandary as couples who were separated by the thortles.

She fingered the beads. Unlike the wooden ones on her belt, these were smooth stones of many colors. She almost wanted to send them back, but that would hurt Narvil's feelings. She sought him out. "Thank you," she said. "Did you make this?"

He seemed to struggle for the right words. "Yes. I make this."

"Tekuyate. It is beautiful." She bent the necklace to show him the tiny hole in one of the beads. "How did you do this?"

Narvil made hand motions and spoke in Human Talk.

"You drill them?"

"No. I cannot explain. Maybe someday, yes."

The next day at language class, Narvil sat on one side of the circle and Aldan on the other, but neither tried to sit by Fern. She was aware of an undercurrent between them. She caught them grinning at each other and glancing sideways at her, but she detected no rivalry. Did both harbor hopes of marrying her? At the same time? She didn't feel comfortable discussing this with Taran, or even Tira. The only person whose advice she wanted was Andli, but Andli didn't speak English.

* * *

Despite wearing a hat out in the open and spending most of her time in the shade, by now Fern's skin was golden brown. She'd always wanted to get a nice tan, but her mother had discouraged her, saying it would age and damage her skin. With the outdoor life here, tanning was unavoidable, but Fern hadn't seen anyone, even grandparents or weka, with the sun-damaged, leathery skin her mother had pointed out on Earth. The sun had bleached her hair even more blonde, a striking contrast to her darkening skin.

Andli finished Fern's new tunic on the day of the Full Moons. She had her try it on, but didn't allow her to wear it yet. That afternoon, everyone was encouraged to rest as much as possible. After nap time, they bathed and repaired their hairdos. These were more elaborate than usual, and Andli and Rina took much time with Fern's.

When they were nearly finished, Tala and Ara approached and handed Fern a small wooden box. Jorsil stood by the house of the weka, grinning. On the lid of the box was an inlay in the shape of an ahnti leaf. Inside were about a dozen little wooden beads with minute ahnti leaves carved on them. Fern picked up a bead and marveled at the workmanship. She wondered how he drilled such tiny holes without splitting the wood. "Tekuyate," she shouted to Jorsil.

He gestured to Rina, who smiled modestly.

Taran said, "He's giving some of the credit to Rina. The beads were his idea, but she helped him with the difficult work."

So that was why they had been working at the weka's house. While Rina and Andli wove the beads into her hair, Fern debated with herself. Was this a gift from a brother? The manner of delivery was that of a potential suitor. She was afraid to ask, only assured herself she'd seen no women with three husbands.

As the sun went down, people donned their best tunics and ornaments. Still, Andli wouldn't give Fern her new clothes. After supper, Andli finally allowed Fern to put on the new tunic. She wore the belt Aldan had given her and the necklace Narvil made.

As the small moon chased the larger into the sky, the people gathered on the sameg with their musical instruments. The moons gave so much light no fire was needed. Andli and Rina held Fern back until the whole village was assembled, then led her into the circle. "Ooh" and "Ah" moved through the crowd like a wave. Blushing, Fern realized the women were presenting their new daughter to the village. Although she had no mirror, her beauty was reflected in the eyes of her audience. Fern looked at Tira, half expecting to see envy, but Tira, too, beamed with admiration.

Children began to pass around cookies and Ara handed one to Fern. She found a seat to hide her awkwardness. A musician struck a chord and music began. Fern recognized the tune—an Irish jig! Her father came to mind. His parents had told him little about their ancestral homeland. Attempting to discover his roots, he'd learned Irish dances and taught them to his daughters.

Fern stuffed the cookie into her mouth, jumped to her feet, and joined the other dancers. They observed her movements and tried to copy them. The pace of the jig caused many missteps and much laughter. Fern saw a woman throw up her hands, giggling. Narvil tapped Fern on the shoulder and said, "Please show us." Fern waved to the musicians to slow their tempo, then demonstrated the steps until the others caught on.

After this, dancing came easy for Fern. Seeing others struggle with new steps, she no longer felt embarrassed when her feet tangled. She danced the night away, every couple's dance with a different boy. Her hair fell apart and the beads scattered. Jorsil, her partner at the moment, smiled and helped her pick them up. She gave them to Andli for safe-keeping. Jorsil took the liberty of running his fingers through her hair, ostensively to save any remaining beads. A thrill rippled through her as her hair fell down her back. She glanced at Andli and Rina to see if they were upset that their handiwork had been ruined, but they seemed happy that she was having a good time.

At breaks between dances, she devoured cookies. Soon she grew tired of sweets and was happy to drink some bitter tea. At midnight, the activity ceased. All eyes watched the small moon move across the face of the larger, making perfect concentric rings.

"This is an extremely rare event," Taran said. "Usually the eclipse is not so perfect." Andli said something which he interpreted with a nod. "It's as though the moons are paying tribute to your joining us on our world."

Elation filled Fern's entire being. She could neither move nor speak. As she gazed up at those perfect circles, she felt rooted in place, standing in the very center of the universe. She let gratitude pour from her for the beautiful tunic, the loving care of her new family, the embrace of the entire community.

Once the small moon separated from the larger one and went on its way, music and dancing resumed and continued until dawn.

CHAPTER 15
FITTING IN

When Fern woke late in the morning, she felt grimy, having slept in her sweaty tunic. Many had gone swimming before retiring, but Fern had been too tired. She took her old green tunic to the pool by her mother's hut, bathed, dressed, and washed her new one. Since Andli and Rina were still asleep, she combed and fixed her hair in one simple braid down her back.

That day, no chores were done except those most necessary. The last of the sweets disappeared and no one took note of who ate them. That night, there was less activity in the sameg than usual, but by the following day, the normal rhythm of life resumed.

After the Feast of the Full Moons, Fern watched those celestial orbs wane, rising later each night just as Earth's moon did, but on separate schedules. The large moon still shone in the early morning hours when the small one seemed to disappear from the sky, emerging a few nights later as a new moon.

On the sameg one night, Fern noticed the faint image of the moon in the arms of its crescent. Her father had called this "Earth shine." What did they call it here? What did they call this planet? Somehow she'd never thought to ask its name. Why? That should have been one of her first inquiries. Why had she been here all this time and not even wondered about its name? The answer came to her. As long as it had no name, it had no reality, like a dream. Did asking its name mean she was now ready for the dream to end? There was sadness in this thought, but her curiosity was strong.

Fern asked Taran, "What do you call this planet?"

"We have no name for it."

"Really? Why?"

"We don't name it, because that would give it a focus that something with no name doesn't have, and it would be easier for us to be discovered."

"What do you mean?"

"By naming it, we might alert our cousins on the thortle world."

"Does their planet have a name?"

"Yes, but we don't use it. Actually, 'thortle' means captor, or enslaver. They don't call themselves that, but we left their name and that of their planet behind when we came here, so it would be harder for them to find us."

"That's weird, for a planet not to have a name."

Taran smiled. "Does Earth really have a name? It didn't, before people realized it was a heavenly body. What does 'earth' mean in English? Soil, dirt, the ground under your feet. The other planets in Earth's solar system were named after gods, even before people knew they were planets, when they thought they were wandering stars."

Fern looked at the shadow of the moon. "So you don't have a name for Earth shine?"

"I guess that's as good a name as anything."

"And the moons aren't named, either?"

"That's right. For the same reason."

* * *

A few days later while Andli and Rina plaited Fern's hair, Tira asked, "What's your favorite color?"

"Blue."

"Good choice."

Smiling, Andli said something and pointed to Fern's eyes.

Tira said, "She's going to make you another tunic."

Fern accompanied Andli to gather the materials and help her prepare them. This time Fern paid closer attention but knew she couldn't duplicate the process without written instructions. Again she lamented the absence of reading and writing materials. She helped Andli set up the loom and did much of the spinning and some of the weaving. She could tell Andli was proud to have such an adept pupil.

Although she still struggled with Human Talk, Fern could understand a few words and follow simple directions. While her pronunciation remained awkward, she began to make simple intentions and needs known. Tira or a member of the language class usually accompanied her on excursions into the forest with a teacher, but Fern depended less and less on a translator.

Taran continued her education in meditation and the psychic arts. Fern had a twofold goal—to wrashiru so she could go home and to project herself in order to read books.

One day Taran guided her into a hypnotic state. "Picture a place high on a hill. A path before you leads down into the forest." She placed herself mentally at the path that led to the waterfall. "Descend a few steps and tell me what you see." She walked down to a shelf of rock and described the vegetation around her. "Focus not on the visual, but inside yourself. This is not a virtual journey, but one into your mind."

She descended to a turn in the path and said, "It's dark here, and warm, comforting. Not really dark, there's light I can't see, only feel."

"Good. Go deeper."

After the lesson, Taran encouraged her to explore her mind on her own. "You have the ability, or you wouldn't be here. You only need to unlock your mind."

She tried to follow his advice but her mind tended to wander. Instead of exploring its depths, she found herself thinking about other things. One of them was meditation itself. Taran seemed to treat meditation as the path to developing psychic abilities. On Earth, she knew, some religions practiced meditation. No one here talked about religion. Why?

Fern had grown up unchurched. Her parents didn't see religion as necessary for a virtuous life. They had no objections to her accompanying her grandparents to church when she visited them, but they themselves did not attend or send the children. Growing up in the South, Fern was surround by people whose religion was an integral part of their lives. Surely her new people had some beliefs or traditions, but what were they?

Before her lesson the following day, Fern asked Taran, "Just what is your religion here?"

He smiled. "You see our 'religion' every day. It's our way of life."

Fern thought about how they'd taught her to ask permission of plants before taking their parts for food or clothing. By habit she now thanked both river and sky for providing water, and the forest for firewood. Before engaging in any task, even such mundane ones as shelling nuts, she joined the others in brief meditation. "It seems like 'giving thanks' is part of your religion."

He nodded.

"But you don't worship the spirits of plants and such."

"No. We don't worship them. We respect them. They are our brethren. All things have what you might call a soul, just as humans do, only less complex. All together, we are the soul of God."

"So, you believe in God?"

"In that context, yes." He paused and took a deep breath. "We are still in the process of developing our religion. It is our understanding of the universe and how to relate to it. We had no religion on the thortle world."

"Oh? Didn't the people who were captured have religions?"

"Yes, but many were so traumatized they abandoned their faith. Even if they didn't, they found no one to worship with. Our beliefs were discouraged, much the way religion is discouraged in Earth's communist countries. We were given only a scientific view of life, which isn't bad, but there's more to the universe than that."

"I wonder if the thortles had a religion."

"We don't know. They revealed very little of themselves to us. But even if they do, they consider humans to be beneath them, much as people of Earth regard cattle. Most people don't teach religion to their animals."

"But what about psychic ability? What does that have to do with science?"

"Everything. It eludes the scientists on Earth, but someday they'll come to understand its importance. The thortles saw psychic abilities as tools they could use, like homing pigeons were once used to send messages on Earth. They didn't see a spiritual aspect to it, and neither did our people when we lived there. When we came here, entire vistas of awareness were opened to us."

* * *

Fern practiced meditation in her mother's hut, sitting in the rocking chair. Here, she felt connected to her mother, her family, her home. Using skills Taran taught her, she chose a quiet mental path and went deep into her mind, to a place where she could reach out.

Every day she tried to contact her sisters but wasn't always successful. Once she managed to project herself into her old school library but was unable to remove a book from a shelf. From there she went to her grandparents' home. Her sisters lay in bed while their grandmother read them a story. Fern strained to listen, but sound was distorted, as though she were underwater. She closed her eyes and relaxed. After a moment, Grandma's voice grew clear, telling a story Fern hadn't heard before. She listened with fascination until her grandmother closed the book and said, "We'll read more tomorrow night."

The following day, Fern tried to repeat the experience, but her timing was off and her sisters were already asleep. Mentally, she sat on the bed beside them. "I can see you. I'm really far away, but part of me is here with you. I love you. I'm glad you're with Grandma and Grandpa. I know they love you and take good care of you." She told them about her new family, her new life. "Please tell them I'm still alive, but I live on a different world. I'll come to visit you whenever I can." Even though she didn't know if they could hear or understand, being with them in this way gave her comfort.

* * *

One day, a young couple entered the village. Andli ran to meet them. The young man threw his arms around her, swept her off her feet, and whirled her around. Both were laughing through tears. Only after he set her down was Andli able to hug the young woman. The other members of the household followed and the couple was introduced to Fern as Andli's oldest son Rufan and his mate Sela. They had been living at the village by the sea with Sela's family. Other relatives and friends wasted little time greeting them, and Fern was left trying to sort out relationships.

She asked Tira, "Why didn't they wrashiru here?"

"Because Sela's pregnant."

"Would that hurt the baby?"

"We don't know for sure, but no one wants to take any chances."

Fern withdrew to her mother's hut, hoping her absence wouldn't be noticed. She'd finally become comfortable with the people of the village, and here was another brother to get to know, and a sister in law. How she longed for a reunion with her own family! She kept a spindle in the hut to occupy her hands at such times. Sitting in her mother's chair, she felt her closeness. Rocking soothed her anxious nerves. Spinning coarse yarn to finer, to thread suitable for weaving, helped focus her mind until her equanimity returned.

Like Andli, Sela was skilled in the fabric arts, so she helped with Fern's new tunic. Although she and Fern couldn't converse, they easily warmed to each other, singing and humming while they worked.

Fern asked Taran what had happened to Rufan's father.

"Autin was a student of Darsan, our geologist. They went on an expedition to mine for stones. Darsan was teaching Autin how to split rock from a mountain when something went wrong. Autin used too much force and the mountain came apart. He was crushed by falling rock." Taran sighed. "Darsan managed to wrashiru, but Autin couldn't. His body was too badly damaged to mend, and so he died. That's how Darsan got that scar on his face. Rufan was only a toddler when it happened."

Fern was silent for a moment. This gentle world harbored danger, after all. "Andli must have been devastated."

"She was. But Sela has chosen to have her baby here, with Andli, so she's very happy. We all are." He beamed. "This will be our first grandchild."

* * *

The next afternoon, Fern came across Rufan and Rina working together. Rufan held a short board while Rina drilled a hole near each end with a black-tipped tool. Then Rufan smoothed the insides of the holes with pumice stone. Having seen nothing resembling a saw, Fern wondered how they had cut the board so neatly.

Tira joined them with a coil of rope. "We're making a swing," she said. "I thought the children would enjoy one. A cousin in the village by the sea made the rope, and Lila sent it with Rufan and Sela."

Fern fingered the rope. It was made of plant fibers twisted tightly together. These fibers were different from those used for garments, longer and more coarse. If the ropes were sent from the village by the sea, Fern surmised, the plant they came from must not grow in the mountains.

They had chosen a tree on the edge of the forest. A group of children eagerly stood by, and Jorsil was already in the tree, astride a sturdy limb. Rufan threw an end of the rope to him and he tied it around the branch. Then Jorsil pulled the rope up, secured the other end, and let the middle drop. Rina cut the rope in half, threaded the ends through the holes in the board, and tied them with large knots.

The children circled the swing in fascination, but no one moved to try it until Tira showed them how. One by one, they swung for a minute or so, then dismounted, laughing and dizzy. "There's enough rope for another swing," Tira said. "We'll hang it on the other side of the tree."

Fern waited until everyone left. Then she sat on the swing and pushed herself gently back and forth. This was a very high swing. She looked up into the tree, which spread arms out on either side as though to welcome swinging children. She pumped herself back and forth, higher and higher, until the leaves caressed her hair, and then her feet. Up, then back down, then up the other side, the breeze blowing her tunic and cooling her face. When she finally dismounted, she found Rondal watching her, wide-eyed, as though he hadn't imagined how high the swing could go.

* * *

Rufan and Sela had been sleeping on the sameg, but since they planned to live here, the village built them a house. They chose an open area between two other houses and the entire village helped set posts, complete the framing, and prepare the finishing work. They notched posts, beams, and rafters to fit together, then lashed them into place with twine.

Dead trees were used for the frame, but more supple wood was required for wattles. Not far from the village, a grove of young saplings grew closely together. Doran chose the healthiest trees, spaced far enough apart for good growth, and marked them. Then his helpers bowed their heads while Rufan asked permission to thin out the grove to build a house for his family. He took out a large knife—a sharp blade of shiny black stone attached to a wooden handle. With this he cut down the trees he needed and everyone helped trim them and carry them to the village.

The saplings were split into thin strips. Fern had never thought about weaving wood before, nor was she aware that between the thatched outer walls and the woven mats inside, the houses were made of slats of wood woven between upright posts. Her mother's hut, intended to be only a temporary structure, was not so solidly constructed.

One morning, Fern noticed Taran next door talking with the weka, who were shaking their heads. Taran opened his hands as though expressing indecision. After more discussion, he nodded and returned to their house, wearing a frown.

"What's wrong?" Fern asked.

"We don't know. The weka have been experiencing a feeling of impermanence, but they don't understand why. They advise finishing Rufan and Sela's house anyway."

Fern felt the old sense of foreboding. "Is Sela in any danger? Or the baby?"

"No. They don't fear for them, but they feel something and said they will put a shield of protection around us all."

While she helped work the wattles through the studs, children collected large leaves that resembled palm fronds. Andli and Sela bundled them to make thatch. Once the wattling was complete, thatching began. Workers lashed the bundles to the wattles and rafters, starting at the bottom and working to the top.

"Why do you need a roof when the weka keep an umbrella over the village?" Fern asked.

"Just in case," Tira said.

"Why aren't we building rooms for children?"

"Those will be added later, as the family grows."

Rina carved designs into the posts. Fern helped Sela and Andli weave mats for the interior walls and floor.

Work on the house took place only after daily chores were done. Even so, within a few days all but the finishing had been completed. Those final touches seemed to take longest. Before the couple was allowed to occupy their new house, the village held a celebration. Sela and Rufan moved their few belongings in and prepared their beds. That night, the whole village sang them to their new home. To Fern, this seemed like a wedding celebration. Tira confirmed that, in a way, it was.

CHAPTER 16
TIME

The next time the large moon was full, the small one was just past new. When the large moon waxed again, Fern wondered if the small one might catch up and they'd be full together, although Taran said they'd go through many cycles first. At the next full of the small moon, the large one lagged behind.

Fern began to wonder how time was measured here. There were no clocks and she had seen nothing resembling a calendar. Things like English class were held at "mid-afternoon" or "just before supper." Everyone except Fern arrived on schedule. At times she was aware of little mental nudgings which weren't quite strong enough to remind her of the class until someone summoned her. The only time she thought to ask Taran about their timekeeping was when he wasn't around.

One day, names of months and days of the week came up in English class. The other students marveled at this strange custom, because they had no such words. She asked Taran to explain.

"We don't segment time like you do on Earth. We see time as flowing. Since we live in the tropics and don't have seasons, we observe the turning of the stars and the phases of the moons. The main division of time we observe is the Full Moons. To express someone's age, we'll say she has passed ten Full Moons. Or to tell when an event happened, we say it was after the fiftieth Full Moons."

"Didn't they measure time on the thortle world?"

"Yes. The thortles had their own system according to their days and seasons. It's curious, but when they became space-faring, they adopted the interstellar time which other races use. That's what was imposed on us. Being artificial, it's in conflict with the rhythms of their world. We don't know how that affected them, but even though our people were confined indoors, we were sensitive to the planet's rhythms. After we came here, we became synchronized with the rhythm of our new world, but we didn't bring the thortles' measure of time with us. Having no experience with a natural calendar, we didn't create one. We just let time flow."

"How long have I been here, Earth time, that is?"

He thought for a few seconds and said, "About six months."

"Do you know what date it is there?"

"Ask me later and I'll be able to tell you."

When he did, to her dismay, she'd missed her birthday. Although birthdays didn't seem to be celebrated here, it hurt that hers had been ignored. Taran picked up on her feelings. "I'm sorry I didn't explain it to you. The Feast of the Full Moons was your birthday celebration. You were honored for having been 'born' to our world."

"But, why didn't you tell me when it was my birthday?"

"Estut miryit. I'm sorry. I didn't understand how important it is to you. We don't celebrate birthdays here. I should explain things to you more. Please don't hesitate to ask me about anything you don't understand. If I'm not around, Tira can help you."

She nodded. But she hated asking Tira about every little thing. And she didn't understand why she felt that way.

So, she was fourteen now. Her friends would soon start high school. She had looked forward to football games, joining the chorus, working on the school newspaper. What else would she miss out on? She'd been absent half a school year already. True, she'd learned a lot, but how much was relevant to her studies on Earth? The longer she stayed here, the further behind she'd get.

More than a year had passed since her encounter with Tira at Disney World. Tira had ruined that birthday for her, and now these people ignored another. Logically, she knew they treated her no differently than anyone else, but that didn't ease the heartache.

She needed to be alone, to nurse her disappointment. Instead of going to her mother's hut for comfort, she walked through the woods until she was tired, then sat against a friendly tree. By now she was beyond crying. She sighed deeply. Someone else sighed! Jumping to her feet, she looked around but saw no one. From above her, in the tree, came another sigh. She peered upward, looking for the source. A gentle breeze sighed among the tree's leaves. Fern couldn't help but laugh.

She recalled the name of this tree—an erguvon. It reminded her of an oak. Not one of Florida's oaks, but of the oak trees that grew farther north, with many limbs stretching out on all sides, easy to climb, provided one could get into the lower branches. Fern glanced around furtively to be sure no one was watching. One bough dipped low enough. She got her hands, then her arms around it, and scrambled up. Another branch was within arm's reach. Cautiously, she stood, holding onto the second limb for balance, and inched toward the trunk. The branches were arranged almost like a spiral staircase, so Fern climbed, nearly to the top.

Unexpectedly, a wind rose and the tree began to sway. Fern gripped the narrowing trunk, suddenly afraid of falling. The wind abruptly ceased and she recovered her balance. Holding tightly, she surveyed the forest and the mountains around her. Here, she could see more than from any other vantage point except the cliff by the lake. And there she couldn't see all the way around. Cautiously, she crept around the bole of the tree. Beyond the tree-covered hills, she glimpsed a conical peak of black rock. She wished she could stay in that tree forever.

Eventually she climbed part way down, to a bough wide enough for her to sit on. She nestled her back against the trunk, as comfortable as in an easy chair, and admired the tree's size and strength, the beauty of its form, its heart-shaped leaves. The squirrels and birds back home would love this tree. She also thought about bugs and was glad there were none here. Her thoughts returned to the birds and squirrels and she realized the tree had no knowledge of them. She pictured squirrels romping on the large branches and skittering up the small ones. She envisioned birds perching on twigs and building nests. As if it knew her thoughts, the tree began to sway gently, even though there was no breeze.

* * *

After this, Fern began to keep track of time by etching on a support post in her mother's hut. Days here were longer than those on Earth. Lacking the math skills to keep track of the passage of time on Earth, at least she could keep track of "months" here. After consulting with Taran, she made seven scratches on the post, the number of times the small moon had passed full since her arrival. She chose the smaller moon because it was quick and eager, unlike the large one which didn't hurry to complete its cycle.

When the small moon became full again, she made another mark on the post. Then she sat in her mother's chair, went into deep meditation, and by ethenos projected herself into her grandparents' house. To her dismay, no one was home. A calendar in the kitchen showed it was July, but there were no markings to indicate which day.

Where would the family be? Mentally, she called out to her sisters and found herself at the state park not far from her grandparents' home. Her sisters splashed in the lake while Grandma watched from the beach. Nearby, Grandpa stood on the dock fishing. Fern hovered around her sisters, wishing she could play with them, until Grandpa approached the shore holding a couple of fish. "Come on, girls," he called. "Let's go home and fry these babies for supper."

Fern hugged each of them and said, "I love you," before going back to her body.

* * *

One day after gathering firewood, Fern crossed the meadow on her way to the village. She glanced over at her mother's grave with thoughts of watering the miaven and saw a group of children around the tree. It had sprouted red flowers! She dropped her wood and ran. The children looked at her and chattered. Fern heard Doran's name. The flowers were actually purplish-red leaves at the tip of each branch, like the bracts of a poinsettia. Still, they looked enough like flowers to bring tears of joy to her eyes.

Taran was at the sameg when she returned with her firewood. She told him about the flowers. He nodded. "Doran has made nuts and roots grow larger to feed us better, but he never thought to make a flower until you wanted some for your mother's burial. Perhaps he'll make more now."

"But how can he do that?"

"With his mind. He talks to plants. He tells them what he wants and the plants do all they can to please him."

Although Fern wasn't convinced that plants have consciousness, she had no other explanation for flowers on the miaven tree. She knew plants could be cross pollinated to select new traits, but this tree had been transplanted, not grown from seed. She had seen Doran sitting before it many times. What was it like to talk to a tree and have it answer back? Her thoughts returned to the erguvon she'd climbed. It seemed to respond when she thought about birds and squirrels in its branches. Had she communicated with the tree or was it only her imagination?

She wished she could discuss such things with her father.

* * *

The more Fern helped Andli with clothing construction, the more adept she became. Gathering reeds and extracting the fibers was tedious, but dyeing them was fun. As she learned what plants and clays to use for pigments and how to process them, Andli allowed her to select colors. Most people found spinning monotonous, but to Fern it was calming. Her first solo project was a blanket for Sela's baby, made with soft yarn on a flat loom. Andli taught her to weave intricate designs into the cloth. Fern had seen demonstrations of spinning and weaving at historical sites back home, but no one used a three dimensional loom like Andli's.

The fabrics were durable. Children outgrew their tunics before they wore them out, so hand-me-downs were a way of life. After her new tunic was finished, the threadbare one was returned to its owner who kept it as a spare.

When Tala received a second-hand tunic from an older cousin, Sela helped Andli make a few repairs and embroider designs around the neck. Once finished, Tala was as delighted as if she'd received a new one. When a garment wore beyond repair, it was cut into usable pieces for towels, handkerchiefs, and diapers.

When Fern's new tunic was ready, Andli used yellow thread to embroider the edges with the fern pattern. Fern felt like the best dressed girl in the village.

CHAPTER 17
TIRIL

Fern was wearing her new red tunic one morning when a handsome young man appeared in the village. Tira introduced him as her brother Tiril. His eyes were the same green as Tira's and Taran's.

"I am pleased to meet you." He spoke perfect English. "I have been living with my mother Lila at the village by the sea. I am honored to have you join our family."

A wave of warmth enveloped her body. Fern was too flustered to make an intelligent reply, only to say, "Tekuyate."

"I plan to travel to Earth and I am trying to improve my English. I would appreciate it if you would correct me if I make any mistakes."

"Sure. I'll try."

He then excused himself and went to join his friends. Fern followed him with her eyes. When she turned back, Tira was staring at her.

Whenever Fern caught sight of Tiril, she grew warm and her heart fluttered. She hoped no one noticed. After lunch, she retired to her mother's hut, but was unable to sleep or meditate. Her thoughts kept turning to Tiril. She sat on her mother's cot, debating what to do, when the doorway darkened.

Tiril said, "There you are. May I come in?"

Heat flushed through her. Every muscle in her body clenched. She managed to squeak, "Yes."

He glanced at the other cot and sat down. "I have to get used to Earth ways before I go there."

Not knowing what to say, Fern asked, "Do you know who made the rocking chair?"

"Yes. My brother Ansil, who lives in the village by the sea, made it. He is a woodworker. Rina and I helped him, because he was pressed for time."

"Does he make furniture for the sea people?"

"No. They do not use furniture."

"Then how did he know how to make a rocking chair?"

"I helped him study a book from your world that showed us how."

A book from her world? Her heart skipped with anticipation. "Where did you get it?"

"We did not get it. We went to it. Do you remember how you visited your sisters? It was similar to that. Taran will instruct you."

Well, maybe there was hope she could get some reading material after all. But how did he know about her visiting her sisters? She set that thought aside and swallowed the lump forming in her throat. "Did you meet my mother?"

"Yes. She was a very nice lady."

Fern closed her eyes to hide tears. Tiril lowered his gaze. She took a deep breath and asked, "Why don't you have furniture here?"

"We have grown accustomed to our way of life and see no reason to change. Besides, we have other uses for our time." He smiled. "You may take the chair to the village if you want to. There is no reason why you should not."

"No, I'll keep it here."

That evening on the sameg, Tiril took his place with the musicians, playing the mandolin she'd seen hanging on the wall in the boys' room. When the dancing began, he laid it down and went to Fern. Holding out a hand, he said, "Will you dance with me?"

The music sounded like a waltz. "I'm not sure I know how to do this."

"It is not hard. Lila taught me and I need to practice. I will teach you."

At first, she tried to imitate steps she'd seen in movies. The results were ungraceful, jerky.

Tiril squeezed her hand and said, "Relax. Let me lead."

She melted into the warmth of his touch. One of his hands held hers, the other rested lightly on her waist. Her hand on his shoulder felt the gentle flow of his muscles beneath his tunic. She responded to his subtle movements and glided across the sameg, feeling less like an awkward teenager and more like a young lady. When the dance ended, he elegantly kissed her hand.

At a loss for what to do next, Fern asked to see his mandolin. Still holding her hand, he led her to where he'd left it. She ran her fingers over the wood, inlaid with various grains and colors, and thrummed the strings, made of good, tough cord.

Tiril said, "Rina did the woodwork. Andli made the strings. Unlike the metal strings you use on Earth, these stretch easily and have to be tuned frequently."

When the music started again, the rhythm sounded familiar—country music. It tugged her heart toward home.

"Do you know how to square dance?" Tiril asked.

"A little."

They joined three other couples. One of the musicians called out words she didn't understand. Tiril smiled. "Join hands and circle left." And so they danced. The calls were very basic, nothing complicated, but the motion drove away her homesickness.

"How do your people know how to square dance?"

"Someone brought it back from Earth. We also have dances from other cultures. I understand you know Irish dances. I would like you to teach me." And so she did.

That night, tired though she was, Fern found it hard to sleep. She got up to use the latrine, and when she passed the sameg, she saw a mandolin resting by someone's head. At least Tiril wasn't sleeping in the house with only curtains separating her room from his.

Later that night, it rained. She thought about the young people on the sameg, and one thought led to another. Girls slept there, too. Tiril was of an age to marry. Although Fern knew she was too young, her body bloomed with young womanhood, and she ached for Tiril.

* * *

The magic of the night yielded to sober daylight. Fern's timidity caused her to evade Tiril, but when English class convened, she could no longer avoid him. When she joined the circle of students, she sat across from Tiril.

"We will speak only English today," Taran announced.

"I need to prepare for my journey to Earth," Tiril said. He looked at Fern. "Lila has taught me much, but I need to speak and act like an American. You have had more years of experience with Earth than anyone here."

"Um, okay."

"Lila told me my English is too perfect."

Fern smiled. "Yes, it is. Too formal. You don't use contractions."

"Yes. I d...don't." He burst into laughter.

The other students laughed with him.

Tiril continued. "Lila said I must learn slang. If you will talk to me and let me practice, I will...I'll be grateful."

Fern hesitated. She'd been a child when she lived on Earth, and slang had been discouraged. What did she know that could help him? "Uh, what do want to talk about?"

"I have...I've read many books, but it...isn't the same as being there. I ...I'll go to Pennsylvania first. Did you ever go there?"

"No." She thought about how close to Pennsylvania she'd been. "I went to Virginia once."

"Virginia. Excellent. Tell me about Virginia."

Fern told him about a vacation in the mountains, one highlight of which was the tour of Monticello.

"Oh, Monticello! That was the home of Thomas Jefferson. Please tell me about that."

Fern described the house and grounds and what she'd learned about the third president. Tiril was interested in her description of the slave quarters and Jefferson's relationship with Sally Hemmings. Fern glanced occasionally at the other students. They seemed to be straining to follow the conversation but no one interrupted, until Taran said that was enough for today.

"Thank you," Tiril said. "You have...you've helped me very....a lot."

* * *

After this, Tiril often joined Fern when she was working. If she was shelling nuts, he'd help. "Tell me, in English, what you are doing." He didn't seem to notice her clumsiness, which his presence made worse. If she was spinning or helping Andli weave, he'd strum his mandolin and sing in a beautiful baritone. Although she understood few of the words, Fern relaxed and enjoyed the music.

Tiril had many questions about customs and practices in her culture on Earth. To her surprise, Fern knew more than she realized.

"Thank you. You're a big help to me."

His English became more conversational. For Fern, it was a relief to converse in her native tongue with someone other than Tira and Taran. Among his many questions, Tiril asked about clothing. "I won't wear Earth clothing until I go there," he said, "but I need to know what to expect. I'll have guidance to dress properly, but it'll be a new experience for me."

One day when gathering firewood, Fern came across Tiril, who was doing the same. The tranquility she usually experienced when alone in the forest was thrown into turmoil. She became too keenly aware of the distance that separated them from the rest of the villagers. When he said, "This is the perfect opportunity!" she was flooded with feelings beyond her capacity to sort out.

He smiled. "What I mean is, would you tell me about the forests on Earth? I've read a lot, but you always fill in things the books leave out."

"What do you want to know?"

"Tell me what you've experienced, how they smell, about the animals."

Having a task to focus on put her at ease. Together, they finished filling their slings while they talked. On the way back to the sameg, she asked, "Why do you want to go to Earth anyway?"

"I'm curious. There are many things I want to learn. I want to study music as it is done there."

"Why didn't you go with your parents and Tira?"

"I could have, but I wasn't ready yet. I had a lot of research to do first."

* * *

Tiril spent much time with Hansa, a pretty young woman about his age who occasionally joined Fern and Andli at work. Hansa was gifted with naturally curly hair. Even when plaited and fastened to her head, little curls worked their way loose to frame her face. Fern couldn't help feeling jealous and began to avoid Hansa, especially when Tiril was with her. One day, Hansa approached her, accompanied by Tira. Through Tira, Hansa asked, "Are you angry with me?"

Fern flushed with shame. Hansa had been nothing but kind to her. Looking for a way out, she lied. "No. You remind me of my mother and I miss her so much. When I see you, I think of her. I'm sorry I hurt your feelings."

Hansa looked more puzzled than satisfied, but replied, "I'm sorry to cause you discomfort. Perhaps time will bring healing."

After Hansa left, Tira said, "I don't think she resembles your mother."

Fern, aching for a confidant, whispered, "Can I trust you to keep a secret?"

"Of course."

"I like Tiril."

Tira laughed. "Why, that's no secret!"

"What do you mean?"

"It's obvious you have a crush on Tiril."

Fern's face fell. "Who knows this?"

"Anyone who's paid attention. Why be ashamed of your feelings?"

"Because I'm only fourteen and he's so much older," Fern stammered. "And I think he's in love with Hansa, and I don't want him to know how I feel."

"Why?"

Fern recalled her parents once laughing about a young medical student who had a crush on her mother, an older, married woman with three children. The young man followed her around at work, called her at home, and blushed when she spoke to him. Fern's parents thought it was funny.

"I don't want him to think I'm a silly little girl."

"He doesn't. But he's not courting Hansa either. She's his first cousin, and they wouldn't be allowed to mate and have children. Besides, Tiril's not looking for a mate right now."

"How come?"

"Because when he goes to Earth he'll be gone a long time. He won't choose a mate until he comes back."

So Tiril wasn't sweet on Hansa. Most likely he thought of Fern as a little sister and spent so much time with her only because he needed to prepare for his journey to Earth. With no brothers or close male cousins, Fern had little experience with boys outside of school. Now she observed how Tira interacted with Tiril and emulated her. As she related to Tiril more as a big brother, she felt more comfortable in his presence. Still, her attraction to him continued to smolder beneath the surface.

CHAPTER 18
TALE OF MOSES AND RILA

Taran had tried to teach Fern the words to the morning song. She struggled with pronunciation and, although he gave her a rough translation, she had a hard time linking meanings to the words. Most mornings, she just hummed the tune, throwing in the few words she could say.

One morning, among the voices on the sameg, she heard Tiril's baritone, singing in English:

> Light from the stars begins to fade
> And gathers in the sleeping east.
> We bade goodnight to cool, dark hours
> And welcome in the bright, warm day.
> Our hearts are filled with gratitude
> For this green world, blue sky and sea,
> And for the sun and moons and stars,
> And for the miracles of life.

Afterward, he apologized, "I couldn't get it to rhyme, like Earth songs usually do, without sacrificing the meaning or rhythm."

"It doesn't need to rhyme. It's beautiful the way it is."

"Thank you. This song was composed by our ancestor Hannah shortly after she came here. She was so overcome by the beauty of the natural world, she wrote poetry. It was she who began the tradition of singing to the rising sun."

Tiril taught her the words. "Until you master Hannah's words, you can sing it in English."

That night on the sameg, Hansa stood to perform and Tiril joined her. Hansa sang a verse of a song, then Tiril chanted in English. While Hansa put the drama of the story into her voice, Tiril accompanied his words with gestures and facial expressions:

> For untold years the Chosen People were
> Enslaved by captors, made to work for them.
> The Chosen Ones had powers the captors craved,
> Yet lacked the power to claim their destiny.
>
> The captors tore the mother from the child,
> The husband from his wife was sent away.
> The lost ones grieved but bonds were stronger made.
> Adversity but made them yearn the more
> For freedom, for their own path to decide.
> From time to time, new captives would arrive,
> Bewildered, stolen from their families,
> And for their powers chosen to be enslaved.
>
> And thus was Moses made a captive man.
> His skin was black and foreign was his speech.
> And from his eyes a fire darkly flashed.
>
> He quickly learned our ways and fell in love
> With Rila, woman handsome, brave, and strong.
> From them, three children were conceived and born
> Before their captors sent them both away.
>
> He pined for her as she did yearn for him.
> In the eternal void each night they met.
> Together, they explored the many stars,
> Until a paradise they came upon.
>
> Then Moses fled his captors, Rila too,
> To come together in their land of hope.
> They walked the sea shore, undisturbed, alone.
> Their captors could not find them in this place.

But paradise was poison to this pair,
And so they perished, lacking food and drink.
Their souls remained, explored their new found world,
Unlocked the mystery of life and hope.

They called their children, "Come and join us now,"
Revealed the knowledge needed to survive.

And so, the Chosen Ones began to come.
Their daughter Martha, Tanil was her mate,
Their children Mosa, Hartha, Rilan, too.
And Abraham, their son, with mate Anli,
And daughter Hannah. Others also came.

The children of Anli and Abraham,
Alas, too young to make the journey here,
Were slain in love by those who'd see them go,
To be reborn, in love, in their new land.

Hansa began another verse, but Tiril shook his head and she stopped. To Fern, he said, "I think that's enough for tonight. What follows is a long list of names and relationships, the genealogy of our people." To the general crowd, he said, "For those of you who know English, I apologize for the poor poetry. Alas, I am no poet, merely a translator."

The few who understood him chuckled. When Hansa translated, everyone else laughed. Tiril gave an elegant bow which brought hearty applause.

He sat by Fern. "I hope you enjoyed it. Hansa and I have been working on it for the past few days. We'll have more for you later, but I'll leave out the list of names."

"Thank you," Fern replied. "I did enjoy it. That's the story of your people?"

"Yes, in part. The song was composed by Metia, the daughter of Hannah, before she and her mate went walking. We call Moses and Rila our First Parents. They were not the first parents of our people as a whole, but they brought us to this planet and gave up their lives so we could live here."

"They died much the same way my mother did?"

He nodded.

"Then they taught your ancestors to adjust to whatever killed her?"

"Yes. You see, the composition of matter here is different than on Earth, or on the thortle world. The molecules have a different alignment—I don't know a better word for it. That is why Moses and Rila, and your mother, were not able to survive. But our First Parents learned how to alter their bodies, to align their molecular structure with what we have here. Moses and Rila learned it too late to save themselves, but they passed the knowledge to their children and the rest of the people who wanted to escape."

"Not everyone came here?"

He paused and his face darkened. "There were some who were content to stay with the thortles, and our secrets weren't revealed to them. It's they, or rather their descendants, that we hide from. The thortles can't find us, unless they happened to stumble across this planet. If they did, they'd find it useless for settlement because of the molecular composition. As long as they didn't discover us here, they would leave. However, our distant cousins who remain with them could detect us, so we shield our minds from them. We don't know if they'd tell the thortles about our existence, but we fear they might."

That old fear of the stars popped into Fern's head. She looked at the night sky. The large moon was new and the small one only a waxing crescent. A million stars filled the void. She worried that she lacked the skill to shield her mind.

As though he knew her thought, Tiril said, "We don't worry about you, because your connection to the people on the thortle world isn't very strong."

Fern had been frustrated by Taran's and Tira's reluctance to talk about the thortles, but Tiril seemed willing. She drew a deep breath. "Is Earth in danger of the thortles invading it?"

"Not really. It's too crowded, with so many animal species, not just humans. And although the thortles consider the people of Earth to be primitive, they couldn't settle there without a fight, and it's not worth the effort."

"What exactly do the thortles want people for?"

"Our psychic abilities. They don't have any. Human beings do, some more than others."

"But what good are psychic abilities?"

Tiril smiled. "The thortles would use us to send messages. Unlike your science fiction movies, radio signals are limited to the speed of light. It's difficult to manage an interstellar empire when communication takes years. Telepathy is instantaneous, not limited by light speed. And we can wrashiru incredible distances. Sometimes a message carries more weight if it's attached to a living body."

Fern tried to wrap her head around what he was saying. "You mean there really *are* civilizations out there that rule other worlds? And they travel in space ships?"

"Oh, yes."

"And sometimes they go to Earth?"

He nodded. "We believe that's where we came from, originally. We are certain Moses came from your own country, many generations ago. He was a slave who escaped and ran to freedom. Then the thortles got him. He resented being enslaved again and wouldn't rest until he found another way to escape."

Fern looked at the people around her. Most had olive skin, dark brown hair, and eyes some shade of green. When she first came here, she thought they all resembled one another, but by now she could discern differences. Some had curly hair, others straight. Faces were not all the same shape. Some noses were broader, or longer, or more aquiline. Some faces were flatter, cheekbones higher. "Your people are a mixture of the races of the Earth," she said.

"We believe so. The thortles like to collect specimens. When they discovered that some humans have psychic abilities, they started taking more of us. They have other intelligent captives, from other worlds, and life forms from many places, but these are kept in zoos. They're merely curiosities. The thortles won't take hostages from other space-faring peoples, psychic or not, because they fear retribution. Unfortunately, Earth is not developed enough to come to the rescue of its kidnapped citizens."

Fern pondered all this.

Tiril went on, "Moses explored the thortle world by ethenos and tried to find a way to escape. Finally, he decided that even if he could get out of the hive, he wouldn't be safe anywhere, so he explored other worlds. He tried to find Earth, but the universe is a big place. Then he came here."

Tiril looked up at the night sky. "Those who initially came here after Moses and Rila were very brave, in more ways than one. On the thortle world, we lived in a hive, an artificial environment, totally enclosed, and we were never allowed outside. We know they have outdoor spaces, plants and animals, but we know very little about them. The thortles didn't see fit to educate us beyond what we needed to know in order to serve them. Curiosity was definitely not encouraged. We were fed and kept safe and comfortable so we could work, and that's all. Most of our people had never been outdoors. To come here, where they had to live in and off nature, took a lot of courage."

Fern tried to imagine being inside all her life and suddenly coming here. It had been hard enough for her to adapt, and she was used to being outdoors. "Taran and Tira don't like to talk about the thortle world. Why?"

"Both have bad memories of that world."

"Bad memories? Have they been there?"

"Not in this life. Their memories are from previous lives."

"Previous lives?"

He nodded.

Both fell silent. Reincarnation, Fern thought. Was it real? She had no memory of any previous life. Did Tiril? She thought about asking him, but his attention was elsewhere, watching the dancers. One foot jiggled with the music.

"Do you want to dance?" she asked before realizing this could be taken as an invitation rather than the dismissal she intended.

In return, he said, "If you'll join me."

She danced until she was tired, first with Tiril, then with others, including her old suitors Aldan and Narvil. Then she sat and watched. She knew dancing wasn't an act of courtship here, as everyone danced with everyone else, male and female alike, but perhaps because of her background, dancing with Tiril seemed special. Maybe she should tell him how it was on Earth. She watched Tiril dance with Hansa. Then the two sat together in conversation. With a sigh, Fern rose and went to bed.

* * *

Returning from chores one day, Fern found Taran cutting Tiril's hair, using a knife since they didn't have scissors. Tiril said, "When I go to Earth, I have to fit in."

Hansa sat nearby, working the strands of discarded hair into an elaborate design. Fern had noticed other decorations made of fibers she didn't recognize. Now she knew what they were. She looked closely at Hansa's handiwork.

"Yes," Taran said. "Hair is highly valued as a craft material. Sometimes when people are ready to die, they give their hair. You would be surprised what wonders Hansa and Andli can do with it."

Fern thought about the lock of her mother's hair that Andli had saved and woven into a medallion. But she had removed only one lock, from a place Fern hadn't noticed. That golden hair would have been quite a prize. Fern was grateful that no one had suggested cutting it off.

CHAPTER 19
THE ROCK FIELDS

Because she didn't understand the language, Fern was often unaware of plans being made around her. The next day, she found Andli and Tiril weaving on a small loom with strong cord. "She's helping me make moccasins," Tiril explained. "Tomorrow I'll accompany Darsan on an excursion to the rock fields. Would you like to go, too?"

"Sure. Where are the rock fields?"

He gestured across the river. "About a half day's walk in that direction."

Fern had not traveled that far. "Why are we going?"

"To collect rocks for knives and other purposes. You'll need some moccasins."

Andli motioned to Fern and spoke the word for "observe."

Fern watched closely as they fashioned the sole, removed it from the loom, and restrung the loom with more cord. She worked on the next sole while Andli helped Tiril weave the upper. Rina brought a crock of sticky liquid which they put the finished shoes in.

"We'll soak them for a while, then let them dry," Tiril said. "That will toughen the fabric. Rocks can be hard on the feet."

Andli restrung the loom to accommodate Fern's feet. When her moccasins were completed, they received the same treatment.

The following morning, Andli made sure Fern had her hat and gave her a water bottle made out of a thick, hollow stem that reminded Fern of bamboo.

She started to put on her moccasins, but Tiril said, "Not yet. We'll save them for the rock fields." For lunch, they wrapped skri in leaves and stowed it in pouches fastened to their belts. The others in the party, including Narvil and Darsan's student Tirna, made similar preparations, but no one carried tools, which Fern thought was curious.

Narvil walked with Fern. "Help me practice English," he said. She would have preferred Tiril's company, but he walked with Darsan and Tirna. They followed the river upstream and climbed into an area Fern had not yet explored.

By late morning, they reached the edge of the forest. Before them spread acre upon acre of black rock. Miles ahead rose black mountains. One had a definite conical shape. "Is that a volcano?" Fern asked.

Narvil looked puzzled. "I not understand word."

Tiril stood close enough to hear. "Yes, it is."

Darsan began to speak.

Tiril said, "He's explaining where we're going. He knows of a vein of rock that we use to make knives. I'm sorry, but I don't know the English name of the rock." He translated Darsan's lecture about volcanic activity and how the rocks were formed.

The land was barren as far as Fern could see, strewn with a layer of rough black rocks that looked like they could have fallen from the sky.

"Darsan says these are remnants of an ancient explosion," Tiril said.

Upon closer look, Fern could see veins of whitish rock in some of the mountains, and streaks of red. "Why are they different colors?"

Tiril asked Darsan a question but didn't translate his answer. "He's explaining it, but I don't know the English words. The rocks consist of different minerals, and some were formed at different temperatures."

"How does he know so much?"

"He studies and observes."

"Does he read books from Earth?"

"No. He doesn't read any of those languages. Earth is not the only source of knowledge."

Darsan finished talking and began to descend the hillside. The group followed.

When they reached the bottom and Fern had time to catch her breath, she asked, "Are any of these volcanoes active?"

"No. We believe them to be extinct, or at least dormant. Otherwise we wouldn't have built the village so close to them."

By noon, they reached a huge slab of stone which long ago had slipped off the mountain and lay propped against another boulder. A trickle of water flowed underneath. The space was cool and roomy enough for everyone to get out of the sun. They paused long enough to drink, eat, and refill their bamboos.

Fern wished she could take a nap in the shade. She compared the bleak terrain to the lush vegetation she'd seen in pictures of Hawaii and other tropical places that had volcanoes. "Why isn't anything growing here?"

Tiril said, "It's too rocky. Also hot and dry. It takes time for plants to get established."

Darsan collected the leaves they'd wrapped around their skri and put them in his pouch. It was time to move on.

Soon they came to a cave. Inside was cool and dark. Once Fern's eyes adjusted to the dim light, she could see Darsan stroking a shiny black wall. Fern touched it. The rock was smooth and cool and felt like glass. Everyone stood behind Darsan and bowed their heads.

"We're asking the mountain's permission to take some of its rock," Tiril whispered.

Fern nodded. Then Darsan began to speak and Tiril explained, "He has extracted stone from here in the past and the mountain has given him permission to take more. We need to step outside for safety."

Fern hadn't thought about danger being involved. "Is that how Rufan's father died?"

"Yes. They were doing something like this. Darsan is very careful, but mining is dangerous work. Have you noticed the scar on his face? That happened when Autin died. The wound could have been healed with no scar, but Darsan chose to keep the scar as a way to deal with his grief and guilt."

Fern glanced around. "Where is Tirna?"

"She's with Darsan, learning how to split rock."

"But how does he do it? I didn't see any tools."

"With his mind, of course."

At that moment, a loud snap was followed by a tinkle like falling glass. After a minute, Tirna called them back inside. She and Darsan, both unscathed, carefully picked up splinters of black rock, wrapped them in leaves, and placed them in their pouches. Then everyone faced the wall and bowed their heads to thank the mountain. Fern also thanked the mountain that neither Darsan nor Tirna had been injured. As they re-emerged into the sunlight, Darsan approached Fern with a shard of rock which he laid in her hand.

"Be careful," Tiril said. "The edges are sharp."

Fern recognized the stone. It was what they used for knives and other cutting instruments. She thought back to her father's collection of rocks and a geology lesson he had once given her. "I think the English word is 'obsidian.'"

"Thank you. Obsidian. I will remember that."

They took a different route back to the village and crossed a dry riverbed full of stones that had washed down from the mountains. Tiril said, "We'll take some of these home. We need pumice for smoothing surfaces, and stones the right shape and size for grinding." He explained specifically what to look for.

Fern, who had grown up in Florida where the only rocks came from limestone pits, was fascinated by the variety. She gathered the most colorful stones she could find. Tiril cautioned her, "We aren't collecting them for decoration." Once the group had gathered what was needed and evenly distributed the rocks to be carried home, Tiril said, "You can take a few for your pleasure, as long as you can carry them."

Fern carefully chose stones of every color, small ones that would fit into her bag. She found one shaped like the egg of a small bird. It was grey with white flecks. She held it in her hand for a minute and closed her eyes. How she missed birds.

Tiril approached. "What did you find?"

She extended her hand. "It reminds me of a bird's egg. I can't remember what bird."

Tiril took the rock and examined it. "Bird's eggs are different colors? I didn't know. I thought they were all white." When he handed it back to her, it was warm from his hand.

Narvil approached with a few colorful pebbles. "Please help me find these."

"For jewelry?" Fern asked.

Narvil looked puzzled until Tiril explained "jewelry" to him. "Yes," he said. Soon his pouch was full.

Before they left the wadi, they thanked it for the rocks they had taken. By the time they reached the forest, Fern's burden became heavy but she didn't complain. Her toes poked through holes in her moccasins. When the others discarded their ragged footwear, Fern did the same.

That evening, Fern realized she'd been too occupied all day to think much about her crush on Tiril. She hoped she hadn't acted too silly in his presence. It had been nice to spend the day with him. Then she thought about Narvil and hoped she hadn't hurt his feelings.

* * *

The next evening, activity on the sameg was subdued, much like it had been when Fern's mother died, yet everyone seemed cheerful enough. During the night, Fern was disturbed more than once by the adults in the next room moving about and whispering. When she woke in the morning, they were absent from the house.

She found them on the sameg in a state of restrained excitement. Taran grinned from ear to ear. "Sela and Rufan's baby has been born. Her name is Dorba."

"Can I see her?"

"Not right now. They're sleeping."

Later, after Fern returned from gathering wood, Sela sat under her awning, surrounded by family. She called Fern over. Andli was holding the baby. Fern peered down at her little face and chubby arms and

squirming legs. The attention must have disturbed little Dorba, who began
to whimper. Andli handed the infant to Sela. She smiled, produced a
breast, and began to feed her. Fern averted her eyes, but noticed that no
one else did.

* * *

A few nights later, Tiril and Hansa stood up to continue their story. Again,
Hansa sang a stanza and Tiril chanted in English:

> Moses and Rila walked the mountain glens
> And followed rivers down to sea and shore.
> That's where their children chose to make their homes.

> So, naked did they come to our new world,
> And learned the skills to build, to spin, and weave.
> The forest gave abundant food to eat.
> The mountain gave them fire to cook the food
> And keep them warm long nights and frosty days.

> The youngest child of our first parents, Hannah,
> Too young to mate, decided to explore.
> Her body slept. Her consciousness would fly
> O'er mountain, sea, and forest. She would seek
> The beauty and the wonders of our world.
> Then she would tell the people all she found.

> But one night, Hannah bid the people wake
> And flee their homes: calamity had come.
> The sea withdrew and rose to giant heights
> And swept away all they had worked to build.

> Far up the mountain everyone then fled
> Until the mountain shuddered, roared, and spewed
> The fiery rivers down to burn the sea.

Then Hannah led the people far away
To warmer, gentle lands in our new world.
Where fiery mountains slept and sent forth only
The streams' and rivers' warm and healing drink,
Where food was plenty, life was kind and sweet.

But Hannah missed the sea and chose a mate
With whom she followed rivers to the sea.
In time, companions also joined them there,
And so our people are not one but two.

At this point, Tiril smiled at Hansa and the audience. Then he spoke first and Hansa sang after him:

And Tiril am I, the son of Taran, Lila,
Daughter of the people by the sea,
Who sought a mate among the mountain people.
But Taran loves the mountains, she the sea,
And so the son of both homes have I been.

Tomorrow, will I journey far away
To seek the land of our First Father's birth.
And so tonight I bid farewell to all,
Until the many years see my return.

His bow this time was more modest. Fern was too stunned to applaud. She didn't know his departure was so imminent, and she wasn't emotionally prepared. When Tiril joined her, rather than thanking him for the story, she said, "So, you are leaving tomorrow?"

"Yes. I'm ready. I wanted to wait until the baby was born. And my English is good, is it not?"

"Yes." She barely kept the quiver out of her voice. "But you are still so formal in your speech. People may think it odd."

"Am I not odd? How many people from another planet did you know when you lived on Earth?"

She tried to laugh. "Not many. But you won't tell people where you're from, will you?"

"Of course not. They'd think I was crazy."

Fern swallowed. "When will you go?"

"Very early. Before dawn."

Before dawn? "So you actually leave tonight!"

He nodded.

"I wish I could go, too." Tears fell. Stifling a sob, she blurted, "Take me with you!"

"I would if I could."

"You can. I brought my mother here."

"Then you have the power to take yourself back."

"But I've tried. I really have."

"There's a reason why it hasn't worked. Perhaps you have a purpose here. This may be where you belong."

"I don't feel that way. I feel like such an oddity here."

"We all are oddities. That's why we're here. Our ancestors were oddities. That's why they were captured in the first place." He grinned at her. "So you fit right in."

Without thinking, she threw her arms around him. "I will miss you."

He held her for a few minutes, and his embrace was so sweet. He patted her back and said, "I'll miss you, too."

"Will you do something for me? Check on my sisters. And my grand-parents. I wish you could tell them where I am and that I'm okay."

"I'll check on them. As for telling them anything, well, we'll see." He gave her a brotherly kiss on the forehead before releasing her from his arms.

* * *

After a good crying spell in her mother's hut, Fern tried to find Tiril, but no one could tell her where he was. She thought maybe she could "hitch" a ride back to Earth, much the same way she and her mother had hitched a ride here with Taran and Tira. She decided to get some sleep first and wake early, well before dawn.

She woke during the night and noticed Tira was not in her bed. Only Andli was in the front room, sitting quietly on her pallet in deep meditation. Fern went to her mother's hut. The large moon shone through the hole in the roof. She fingered the post where she kept track of time. She'd known Tiril about two months by the small moon. It seemed longer, like she'd always known him, and now he was leaving. She spent the rest of the night in meditation. She tried to sense Tiril's presence, but a feeling of trepidation held her back. What was wrong? Was Tiril in danger? Or was she afraid of dissolving her own body? Could anything go wrong with wrashiru?

Fern didn't know when he left. She woke in the gray dawn, unaware she'd fallen asleep. When she returned to the house, Tira and the adults were sleeping. On the sameg, people were preparing breakfast. Tiril was conspicuously absent. Fern suspected Tira had been part of a sending-off party to which she hadn't been invited. This hurt, even though she knew her lack of mental discipline could have been a hindrance, or worse, harmful to Tiril.

When Taran woke, she asked, "Is Tiril on Earth now? Is he safe?"

"Yes, and yes."

"I guess you, and some others, were there to help."

"That's right. Wrashiru on this planet, say between here and the village by the sea, is almost routine, but to go to Earth, especially with the physical changes one has to make, is more difficult. To ease the process, we support the person mentally."

"Exactly how is it done? I mean, if I had been there, what would I have seen?"

"You wouldn't have seen anything. Your eyes would have been closed. We all sat in meditation, focusing on Tiril and his needs, while he went into a deep trance. Our friends on Earth were doing the same, steering him in the right direction. When we were aware he was safe at his destination, we relaxed."

"So, one moment he was there, and the next—poof!—he was gone?"

He smiled. "Something like that. Only he's not 'gone.' He's on Earth. Space is not linear. All places are one, except in the conscious mind, which defines space."

"I guess I wouldn't have been much help."

His smile was kindly. "You could not have helped this time, but in the future, you will become a great asset."

At least she hadn't been given up on as useless. "So he's safe? You're certain?"

"Yes. Quite certain."

CHAPTER 20
BARRIERS

After Tiril's departure, Fern couldn't get him out of her mind. Her heart ached in ways it never had before, as much as her longings for family and home. When she visited her sisters by ethenos, she toyed with the idea of looking for Tiril. Would he be able to detect her? Maybe he'd be annoyed. It might be an invasion of his privacy. She decided not to.

Some days Fern had little appetite for the inevitable skri, kirrib, and leni-trus. Although she'd grown up in a subtropical climate, she got tired of sweating so much and didn't always feel like bathing. She missed air conditioning. She grew bored with the nightly entertainments on the sameg and found herself longing to watch TV. She yearned, especially, to read a book.

Some nights she couldn't sleep. After a lying in misery for hours, she'd go for walks. One moon or the other was usually shining. She'd scan the skies, wondering which star was Earth's sun, but she didn't recognize any of the constellations her father had taught her.

Through the trees one night, she spotted a big blue star. Her excitement mounted when, not far away, she saw another. Hoping she'd found Orion's belt, she hurried to the meadow where the sky afforded an unobstructed view. But there was no third blue giant. Depending on where she was in the universe, the stars of Orion's belt, or any other constellation, may not line up the same way as when viewed from Earth.

The next day, she asked Taran if he knew where Earth's sun was and whether it could be seen from this world. He didn't know. "You see the universe as linear. We don't. To us, all space is one, and Earth is just next door, so to speak."

His words brought no comfort. She had no idea if she was even in the same galaxy as Earth. Yet the next time she used ethenos to visit her sisters, she conceded Taran was right. Although separated by undetermined distance, she could put herself mentally in the same room as her loved ones

She renewed efforts to wrashiru. Some days she meditated three or more times. Concentrating on space as "one," she tried unsuccessfully to project herself outside her mother's hut. But wrashiru leaves one's clothes behind. Perhaps this was her reason for failure. So she meditated outside the hut and tried to put herself inside. Then she worried about setting herself in the same place as the chair or cot, which would be disastrous. She asked Taran.

He smiled at her. "Don't worry. You have control over your own movements. It's not like being 'beamed up' on Star Trek, where a machine is doing it to you. It's good you're making these efforts, but perhaps you're trying too hard. It'll come in its own time. Focus on exploring your mind, then you'll find your way."

But the more she explored her mind, the more she found it to be an untidy tangle of cluttered passages and dead ends. One day, rather than exploring, she just let it be. This time, she had a new experience, a sensation of her body becoming immense, as though it would fill the universe. This was not her body but her larger self. Looking inward, she saw her mind as something minute, filled with color, like a child's toy. A childlike delight emanated from it. She looked outward and perceived unlimited possibilities. But the way was blocked by a barrier she was unable to cross.

Fern emerged from this meditation with a sense of well-being deeper than she'd experienced before. Again and again, she tried to achieve that state. Sometimes she was successful, more often not. Always, she ran into that barrier.

When she discussed this with Taran, he was pleased. He encouraged her to keep trying but not to focus on the barrier. "It will resolve itself."

So she explored the barrier without trying to cross it. One day she recognized it as fear. Without consulting Taran, she surmised it was fear of the unknown. Later, the barrier seemed to dissolve somewhat, or recede. Then she became aware that the fear was not of the unknown after all, but of something known that her mind shielded her from. She continued her meditations with less anxiety over the barrier, but with trepidation about what her mind was protecting her from.

* * *

As a child on Earth, Fern had enjoyed picking up words and phrases from other languages. In middle school, she took Spanish. Yet despite her best efforts, she made little progress with Human Talk. The English students learned her language faster than she learned theirs. Although she knew the names for many things and understood greetings and simple requests, to put words into a conversation remained beyond her. The structure and pronunciation were so foreign she was easily frustrated. It didn't help that there seemed to be no logic to the language. The word for "I" was "ta" and "love" was "aloa" but to say "I love you" was "esmilu tefi."

One day Rina sent her to Taran's father, Hatir, to borrow a knife. Fern was unable to pronounce the word or make her request known. She was met with a quizzical look until she drew a picture of the knife in the dirt. Hatir smiled patronizingly and handed it to Fern, who returned home in tears.

Taran tried to comfort her. "The Earth languages all have a connection, however ancient, but this language was developed by a very alien race. It would be easier for you to communicate with a cockroach than a thortle, because at least you have a common history. While I was on Earth, I studied ancient languages and cultures, trying to find vestiges of our origins. But ...I digress."

He went on. "How long did it take you to learn English? Two years to be able to ask for a cup of water? Three or four more years before you could read? Have you totally mastered English now? Weren't you still getting vocabulary lessons in school? It'll take you a long time to learn this language. Be patient. When others smile at your mistakes, they don't intend to criticize. On Earth, didn't you find toddlers amusing when they tried to talk?"

Fern nodded. "I guess I'm talking on the toddler level."

This gave her an idea. That afternoon when the small children were playing, she joined them and sang children's songs to them in English. They loved it. The next time, she taught them to play Ring Around the Rosy, and later, Duck Duck Goose. From the toddlers she picked up words, phrases, and songs in Human Talk. She wasn't sure if she was learning the actual language or baby gibberish, so she was careful not to repeat things around older people.

Yet Fern felt comfortable using "baby talk" with Andli. When she spoke correctly, Andli would nod encouragingly, and Fern could take her gentle correction without shame. Andli seemed to know Fern's feelings and needs. They could communicate without language.

Fern had learned to read others' gestures and facial expressions. She couldn't always glean the substance of a conversation, but she could understand the emotional content. Often she could pick up on emotions without looking at the person. One day Fern felt a wave of contentment pour through her and caught Andli smiling at her with loving pride. Later, when Andli wasn't looking, Fern projected love and gratitude toward her. Andli turned and hugged her. This actually spooked Fern enough to stop her from trying it again.

However, the next day, she inadvertently did something similar. Hatir asked her to help him take several small children to collect firewood. Fern was not in a good mood, but she agreed. The group included Tandil and Gresin, two of her toddler friends. Instead of gathering wood, the boys kept chasing each other. Hatir admonished them several times and Fern gently tried to redirect them.

Once the slings were loaded, Fern hoisted hers onto her back and was trudging homeward when Tandil ran in front of her, causing her to trip and fall. Her wood scattered. Physically, she was not hurt, but her ego was bruised. She turned away to hide her anger, but she muttered, "You stupid little brat."

Immediately, Tandil fell on his face and began to cry. Hatir picked him up. When Fern saw the bloody scratch on the boy's cheek she ran to him, saying, "Estut miryit," but Tandil refused to accept comfort from her. After Hatir tended to the child, he silently helped Fern pick up her wood. His face appeared serene, but Fern could feel his disappointment and disapproval.

After she returned to the village and stowed her firewood, Fern ran to the refuge of her mother's hut. Here she tried to sort out what happened. So Tandil had tripped and fallen. She hadn't touched him. Why did she feel responsible? While she wrestled with guilt and regret, she heard a footstep and Taran's voice, "Fern?" He stood just outside the door.

"Yes."

He came in and sat down. "What happened to Tandil?"

She blurted out, "They kept running and wouldn't stop. He tripped and fell. I didn't do anything to him." These words escaped before she realized she was making excuses for something she intended to pass off as an accident.

But when she looked up, Taran had a small smile on his face, not the look of reproach she expected. "But what did you *think* at him?"

Fern hung her head. "I called him a stupid little brat." After a moment she added, "And I wished he'd trip like I did. And he did."

Taran's smile broadened. "What have you learned from this?"

"How is it possible? I didn't do anything to him."

"You have a powerful mind. You need to control any destructive thoughts. And I'm not telling you anything you don't know."

How did he know her internal thoughts and feelings? Fern felt more naked than she would have unclothed. "But aren't my thoughts my own? Don't I have any privacy in my own mind?"

"Of course you do. But when you project them like that, you might as well yell at the top of your lungs."

Fern shook her head. "It wasn't like that back home."

"Yes, it was. You weren't tuned into it."

Fern was silent for a moment. "Do I really have the ability to hurt someone?"

"Yes, you do. But you also have great capacity to help, and you have a good heart. Let that guide you."

"But what if I don't want anyone to know what I'm thinking?"

"You have that right. No one will intrude on any thoughts you wish to hide."

After this, she hid her thoughts by erecting a mental barrier around herself. As a result, she could no longer "read" others, but she tried not to care. Losing this connection brought back the sense of empty isolation she'd felt after her mother died. She missed her family more than ever, yet the barrier interfered with her checking on her sisters. The last time she'd visited them, Grandma was baking pies for Thanksgiving. Soon it would be Christmas. The ice storm had struck in January. Then the fire. She'd been here nearly a year, yet she was no closer to going home.

Fern continued to meditate, trying to wrashiru, but she ceased her studies with Taran. She drifted through her days with little pleasure. As though they sensed this, the toddlers left her alone. She continued to be a popular dance partner but otherwise the young men no longer sought her company. Occasionally, she caught a look of concern on Andli's face. Only spinning and weaving brought comfort because no social interaction was necessary. She could focus on the skill of her hands and ignore what troubled her mind.

Another change came to her dreams. The evening music stopped following her into sleep. Dreams about her family used to have happy endings, but no more. She'd wake, terrified, to the roar and smell of smoke. She became aware that her openness to others had been a safety net for her psyche, but she stubbornly continued to value her privacy above all.

* * *

One morning, as she sat down to breakfast, Fern noticed several people, including Doran, Andli, and her brother Olan in front of the house next door. Fern turned a querying eye to Taran.

"During the night, Nasi left her body. We will have a burial today. Eat your breakfast, then go to Andli. As a weaver, your help is needed."

While she ate, people of all ages came and went next door, and Fern tried to sort out relationships. Nasi was Andli's and Olan's great-grandmother, also Doran's. Small groups of her descendants visited her house. Some carried coils of vines or baskets of leaves.

Fern remembered her mother's funeral. At the time, Tira told her they digressed from their usual practices to give her mother a burial according to Earth customs. What were these people's traditions? If she were patient, she would find out, but Taran was available. "On the thortle world, did you bury your dead?"

Taran set down his kirrib. His face transformed into a brewing storm. Then he drew a deep breath and calmed himself, but his voice was like ice. "No. They disposed of our dead for us. They put the bodies on a compost pile, or fed them to carnivores in their zoos. Sometimes, life still remained in the body."

Now Fern was sorry she'd asked.

Taran tried to smile. "Please forgive me. Some memories hang heavily on the soul." He sighed. "On that world, new captives told about the customs of their own cultures, but of course we weren't able to put them into practice. Moses told us his people buried their dead, so that's what we do here."

After breakfast, Fern approached Nasi's house with trepidation, hoping she wasn't required to view the body. To her relief, no one asked her to. Andli had constructed a frame for the burial basket out of thick vines. Fern helped her finish it with smaller vines and reeds. No living materials were used, which made them hard to work with since they were brittle and broke easily. As a result, the finished basket wasn't going to look as nice as Andli's usual work. Fern reassured herself that it didn't matter. The basket would be used only once and buried in the ground.

Fern searched Andli's face for indications of grief but saw only a tranquil sorrow. Nasi had no living mate. Her son Torbil sat in the doorway, deep in meditation. Neither of Nasi's daughters lived in the village. One was walking and the other lived in the village by the sea. When Tira arrived with a basket of leaves, Fern whispered to her, "Will her daughters wrashiru here for the funeral?"

"No, it's not necessary. They're here in spirit."

She looked into Tira's basket. It was full of brown leaves that had been picked up off the forest floor. "They used green leaves for my mother."

Tira nodded. "Yes. We thought fresh leaves would give you more comfort, and the trees agreed." She helped Fern and Andli line the basket with leaves.

When they were finished, Nasi's grandchildren carried the basket into the house. "We can go now," Tira said. "Our presence isn't required until burial time."

Later, Fern watered the miaven tree on her mother's grave. Next to it was a freshly dug hole the size and shape of the funeral basket. Fern sat by the tree and relived that awful day when her mother died. At least Nasi was old. Fern didn't know her well, but she had liked her and would miss her. She looked at the purple-red flowers that covered the miaven tree. Her mother would have liked them. Nasi might, too. She wept for both.

Towards evening, Doran, Olan, and two of Nasi's grandsons emerged from the house with the basket containing her body. Torbil and his mates followed, and the rest of Nasi's descendants fell in behind. Andli beckoned Fern to join them. The remainder of the village completed the procession to the meadow, softly chanting. Fern recognized some names—they were reciting Nasi's ancestry.

The basket was lowered into the grave. The chant turned to Nasi's mates, her children, her grandchildren, their children, and their grandchildren. As each name was sung, that person put a spade full of dirt into the grave. For those who were absent, at the sea village or walking, another family member supplied the soil. Fern was surprised to hear her own name. Tira handed her the spade. After contributing her shovelful, Fern went to the miaven tree on her mother's grave and asked permission to pick flowers. She looked up to find Doran standing next to her. He nodded and she picked a bouquet.

When the burial was complete, Fern stuck the stems into the soil. Torbil knelt down beside her and gently touched the flowers. Fern felt a wave of comfort and knew she'd let down her guard, but she was glad the flowers brought him solace.

She took the pitcher to the lake for water. A few family members, including Torbil, lingered at the gravesite. He smiled at her while she poured water around the flower's stems.

"Perhaps you have started a new tradition," Taran said.

* * *

Nasi's burial dredged up memories not only of Fern's mother's death, but also her father's. Her last glimpse of him, sitting by the hearth, still haunted her. The vague apprehension she'd felt at that time morphed into a sense of impending doom, which she couldn't shake.

Days later, she discovered she'd missed Christmas. She'd missed watching her sisters sing carols, decorate a tree, open presents. Did they have a merry Christmas or were they still wrestling with grief?

Well, she didn't have a merry Christmas, or any Christmas, for that matter! Taran had promised to tell her these things, hadn't he? She ran through the woods, making a wide detour around the village, to her mother's grave where she threw herself on the ground and poured out all her disappointment, anger, and pain.

Andli came to her and held her while she cried. When Fern became aware that Taran was there, too, she looked up at him and shouted, "Why didn't you tell me? I missed Christmas!"

"Fern," he said gently, "I thought you were keeping track of time."

She looked away. The flowers on the little miaven tree on her mother's grave shone through her tears. As she gazed at it, a few petals dropped. Maybe it needed water. "Excuse me," she said. Andli released her. Fern grabbed the pitcher and ran to the lake. When she returned, Andli and Taran were gone. She was glad. More than comfort, she needed to be alone. She also watered the blossoms on Nasi's grave. Her attentions to the flowers helped ease her anguish, but sadness continued to cloud her days.

Every day, she watered Nasi's flowers and removed the withered ones. Finally, only one remained and showed no signs of fading. She tugged on it ever so gently and found it had rooted itself in the soil. She ran to find

Doran and, using what words she knew, thanked him. He told her it had been her loving attention, not his, that induced the little tree to take root. His words warmed her for the moment, but part of her sensed that the tree was doomed, that her efforts would never bear fruit.

Back home, it must be January. The anniversary of her parents' deaths. She went to Taran. "I've been here a year now, Earth time, haven't I?"

He nodded.

That night, Fern tried to project herself into her grandparents' cozy living room, desperate to see her sisters, but the self-imposed barrier held her back. She spent most of the night in tears and overslept the next morning.

That day, Doran took Fern into the woods and led her to a small stream. A clump of ahnti grew here. She occasionally gathered the leaves for kirrib. Their taste was bland but helped offset the spicy flavors of other plants. There'd been little rain for several days and the stream was dry. Fern was dismayed that the ahnti leaves were shriveled. The plants looked dead.

Doran performed his usual meditations to the plant, picked a dry leaf, and offered it to Fern. "Taste this." The nutty flavor surprised her. Doran pointed to something Fern hadn't seen before, a ripe, unopened seed pod. She'd seen green ones on ahnti plants, but they usually dried quickly and burst, releasing their tiny seeds. Doran picked the pod, placed it in his pouch, and they returned home.

Taran met them at the sameg and said, "The ahnti plant is very useful. The leaves have high nutritional value, even though they have little taste, but the flavor comes out when they dry. It enhances other flavorings. We collect the roots and dry them to a powder to use in bread dough. It works similar to the way wheat gluten does, helping the dough hold together and rise.

"Ahnti is also used for medicine. Doran makes a tea from the entire plant, including the seed pods. It has a strengthening effect for the sick or injured, also for the very old or anyone suffering grief, and we give it to those recovering from wrashiru. We seldom find a seed pod that's mature but not yet open. So, whenever you find one, bring it to Doran. Be sure to ask and thank the plant, of course."

Doran approached with a fresh cup of tea.

Taran nodded at Fern and said, "Drink."

The tea eased Fern's melancholy and she took a longer than usual nap that afternoon. That night she went to the sameg by habit but sat listlessly, refusing offers to dance. Without a word to anyone, she went to bed but faced another sleepless night. The next morning she woke with a headache and little appetite. Doran fixed her more tea, but she felt worse as the day progressed. Mentioning this to no one, she pushed herself to do her usual chores and avoided social interaction.

By nightfall, she was feverish and hurt all over. Stumbling to the creek, she bathed in the warm, mineral-rich water. It soothed her but left her too weak to walk. She staggered to her mother's hut and curled up on the floor.

She dozed off and half-woke to a cacophony of rude noises squawking in her brain. Unable to sleep, she couldn't fully wake. Andli and Rina found her. Their warm arms lifted her but couldn't dispel those impossible animal sounds. Then she heard Andli's voice, in English, "Fern, let me in." She began to sob and wrapped her arms around Andli. When Andli said, "Shhh," the awful noises ceased and she slept. Singing filled her dreams.

Fern woke on her mother's cot with Andli beside her. The fever was gone. A sticky substance had been applied to her throat, armpits, and groin. Andli helped her up, took her to the stream to bathe, and dressed her in a fresh tunic. Doran brought her a cup of tea. He and Andli helped her walk to the village.

They laid her pallet in the sun and Rina tended to her while Andli and Doran slept. Rina brought her more tea. By midday Fern felt well enough to sit in the shade of the awning. Taran joined her. "I didn't know you could get sick here," she said.

"We have no human diseases, but of course, there are micro-organisms. Most of them are beneficial or don't bother us. You were vulnerable because of your emotional state. With mind control, you can learn to protect yourself. Until then, Andli will keep you healthy, if you let her."

Fern wished she had the verbal skills to discuss her feelings with Andli. She'd grown to love Taran, but she needed a female to confide in. Someone other than Tira.

As she recovered from her illness, she continued to guard her mind but didn't fail to let Andli in. Eventually, she went to Taran and said, "If you don't mind, I'd like your help again, to work on my psychic abilities."

He smiled. "Of course."

CHAPTER 21
THE LIGHT GATHERING

Fern sat with Andli and Rina under the awning in front of their house. While Fern spun thread, Rina carved intricate designs on beads, and Andli worked on a new tunic for Tala. Farsa, the mother of Simbi, one of Fern's toddler friends, joined them with a hat she was making. Little Simbi played nearby with her doll until she grew bored, then she toddled off to the edge of the woods and brought back treasures—leaves, sticks, stones. Each time she wandered off, they sang to her and she sang to them on her way back. Fern could understand only a few words, so she hummed the tune.

Simbi ambled off around a house, out of sight. When Farsa stood up to go after her, Simbi returned, holding Hansa's hand. The women shifted to make room for Hansa, who sat down with her workbasket on her lap. Fern peeked into the basket. Hansa was fashioning something out of strands of dark hair—Tiril's. Fern couldn't tell what it was yet and didn't know how to ask.

A gentle breeze blew the aroma of baking skri their way. Fern's stomach growled but she wasn't hungry enough to get up for some. Still recovering from her illness, she was tired after collecting firewood that morning. The women chatted in Human Talk. Fern caught snatches of the conversation, but not enough to hold her interest.

Simbi roamed off again and the women sang to entice her back. Fern sang along with them in English, "Simbi, Simbi, where do you wander? Simbi, Simbi, please come to Mama." She knew these weren't the exact words, but they fit the tune. The women smiled at her with approval. Simbi returned and squirmed onto Farsa's lap. Farsa was well along in pregnancy and there wasn't enough room for both child and hat, so she set down her work and wrapped her arms around Simbi.

Fern thought of her own mother and longed for her embrace. As though she picked up on Fern's need, Andli leaned over and hugged her. "Tekuyate," Fern whispered.

Across the sameg, Tirna pulled a platter of skri out of an oven. Fern looked at the sun. It was close to lunchtime. She returned her attention to her spinning until she heard Simbi say, "Mmmm." Fern looked up as Tirna set down a half dozen fresh skri wrapped in a cloth. "Tekuyate," everyone said. Fern eagerly nibbled on a biscuit. Someone else must have been hungry, too, and sent Tirna a mental message. Fern was grateful for this.

She watched Tirna cross the sameg to the tetherball court and join the children who were playing. Tala and Ara were among them. Fern recalled how she used to watch her own sisters play. She missed them so much. Since erecting barriers around her mind, she hadn't been able to visit them by ethenos.

That night, she dreamed about them. She was riding a school bus. Her sisters sat in the seat in front of her, talking with their friends. Grandma met them at the bus stop and, on the way to the house, the girls chatted about their day at school. Fern hung on every word. Once inside, Grandma put the six year old down for a nap and the older one began her homework. Fern hovered over her sister who was struggling with a math problem. Oh, that's easy, Fern thought. She pictured the solution. As if she'd heard, her sister quickly erased what she'd written and wrote the correct result. Fern hugged her and said, "I'm proud of you."

Then she went into the bedroom to hug her sleeping sister. "I miss you. Be good for Grandma and Grandpa." Instantly, she found herself back on the unnamed world, relief mixed with longing. She knew it had been more than a dream—an etheric projection—and her sisters were okay.

* * *

A few nights later, both moons were new together. The sameg seemed less crowded than usual. Fern was always a popular dance partner, but every time she started to sit down, someone else asked her to dance. Finally, at a break in the music, she managed to drink a cup of water before Narvil approached her with his hand out. She shook her head and said in broken Human Talk, "I need to rest."

So Narvil danced with Jorsil. Fern scanned the crowd and noticed that more men and boys were dancing together than usual. She couldn't ask Taran what was going on because he was busy dancing with Rina. She looked for Tira, but couldn't find her. Fern was the only adolescent female present.

Hot and sweaty, she drank more water, then she had to use the latrine. The night was very dark. Starlight failed to penetrate the canopy of trees. Fern found the path and groped her way blindly. On her way back to the sameg, a light in the woods caught her attention. "Someone must have a fire there," she thought. Another path led in that direction. It took her near the light but not to it. She picked her way through the underbrush.

In a little clearing, a group of girls were gathered in a tight circle around the light. Tira was there, also Hansa and Tirna. Every girl in the village who had arrived at puberty but not yet mated was present. Fern hid in the shadows and watched. The girls hummed, quietly but intently. They raised their hands slowly over their heads and the hum increased in pitch and volume. The light also increased. Then the girls stepped back, spun around, and broke into song and dance.

Fern's view of the light was no longer impeded. It was not a fire after all. A ball of blue-white-golden light hung suspended about a yard above the ground. Fern froze. She couldn't take her eyes off it. Her body swayed with the music, but her feet remained rooted.

The girls paused and seemed to focus on the light. Then all spoke, as if with one voice, in English, "Let us invite our sister to join us." They turned in unison and faced Fern.

She bolted. In the darkness, she ran slap into a tree and fell backwards. She cowered on the ground, listening. No one pursued her. She crept to her feet, keeping her eyes averted from that light, and searched for the path. She rushed down it as fast as she dared, stubbing toes and scratching arms, before she realized she was going in the wrong direction. The route back to the sameg would take her near the light, so she kept going. Eventually, she found another way that took her back to the village. Instead of rejoining the festivities, she skirted the crowd and went to the fire pit to fix a cup of calming tea. She drank it, wondering what to do next. She wanted to go to her mother's hut but was too frightened to be alone. Instead, she went to bed.

The tea helped her sleep. In her dreams, young women in witch's garb danced around a boiling cauldron. They offered her a cup of their brew. She tipped the cup to her mouth, and it scalded her lips and burned its way down to her stomach, waking her.

Tira was back. "I'm sorry we frightened you," she said. "There was really nothing to be scared of. Nothing was going to harm you."

Fern made no reply but got up and left the house. Maybe she would be safer in her mother's hut after all. Bathing in the warm creek quieted her fears and let her sleep. Another dream. She was shackled in the bottom of a pit, struggling to free herself. On the ground above, a circle of voices sang plaintive melodies, words she didn't understand. Someone lowered a rope ladder. Smooth as satin, inviting, it shimmered with light. Fern reached for it. But when she touched it, a charge of energy shot through her. She gasped and jerked her hands back. Shutting her eyes against the ladder's light, she huddled in the pit as far from the ladder as possible.

She woke, hesitant to open her eyes until she was sure of where she was. Safe in her mother's bed, no pit and no ladder.

When it was light enough to see, she made her way to the sameg. The girls who had been at the gathering in the forest greeted her in English, "Good morning, sister." Fern grumbled, "Salut," grabbed some skri, and retreated to her mother's hut.

The skri formed a clump in her stomach. She sat in her mother's rocking chair and took up spinning, but her hands shook and jerked knots in the thread. She threw down the spindle and rocked frantically, beating her fists on the arms of the chair. Why—just whenever she started to feel at home, like she belonged—why did something like this always happen? "I just don't belong here!" Cramming her fists into her eyes, she cried, "It's so unfair. It's just so unfair. I want to go home." She tried to meditate, to take her mind into that quiet place where she visited her sisters, but her mind jerked in all directions, like a colt that had been stung by a hornet.

Around midmorning, after her misery had wound down to discomfort, Andli and Taran came to the hut.

"Estut miryit. I'm sorry. I'll go do my chores."

She tried to rush past them, but Taran said, "That's not why we came."

"I don't want to talk to anyone."

"No, but you do want an explanation. May we enter?"

She sat in her mother's chair and rocked. They each sat on a cot. Doran showed up with a cup of tea and Rina with Fern's comb and hair fasteners. Fern sipped the tea and allowed the women to comb and fix her hair. No one spoke. Finally, Fern asked, "What was that all about last night?"

Taran said, "I've never been to one of those gatherings myself. There is no rule that males cannot participate, but it seems to work only for females of a certain age." Andli and Rina spoke and he translated, "When the moons are dark, we are drawn to make light, much the way we are drawn to celebrate the light of the Full Moons."

"I thought the Feast was just a party. Like Christmas."

"It is, but even Christmas is more than a party. For Christians, it's a celebration of the birth of Light into the world, in the form of the Christ Child. It's held at the same time of year that the old Europeans celebrated Yuletide, at the rebirth of the sun. And Chanukah, for the Jewish people, the Festival of Light, often coincides with it. It seems to be something inborn in us humans. We had no such celebrations on the thortle world. Captives who brought spiritual practices with them usually found no one who shared them. And the shock of capture usually negated their religious beliefs, so they abandoned them."

Fern was in no mood for a lecture. "It looked like witchcraft."

"In Earth's history there have been similar gatherings of women. Some were considered very spiritual. There were gatherings of men, too. For some reason, those were acceptable, but the women's were often feared, considered evil, and the participants were persecuted. Think about Salem, Massachusetts, in your own country's history. Were you taught to believe that such things were evil?"

She shook her head. "But what about that light? At first I thought it was a fire."

Here, Andli's and Rina's input was needed. Taran translated. "It was a focusing of energy. It helps the young women develop their powers. We don't know why it works only for girls." He smiled. "Maybe it's something found only on the X chromosome. When girls reach puberty, they can band together to do things they're unable to do individually. It helps each girl strengthen her talents. It also helps them to use certain abilities while conscious that are otherwise possible only in meditation. This is important for women, because bearing and nursing children leaves them little time to meditate. The gathering also identifies fire makers. There has to be one in the group to make the light as strong as it was last night."

"Fire maker?"

"Like Alta."

"I thought she only tends to the fire."

"She does. It's easier to keep a fire going than to make a new one, but she has that ability. Each generation, we look for another. It's always a woman. Hannah, the youngest daughter of our First Parents, was inspired by a dream to organize the first Light Gathering, which produced our first fire maker, her sister Martha."

Fern thought for a while. "But you told me to pay attention to my feelings. I got a bad feeling about that last night."

"Examine your feelings."

She did. "It scared the snot out of me!"

"Of course. It was something very foreign to your experience, something bizarre, beyond your belief in what's possible."

Fern nodded.

"You've encountered many such things since you've been here. And you will encounter more. We try to introduce these things to you slowly, to give you time to accept them and adjust, but it's not always possible. We don't want to shelter you to the point of stunting your growth." He paused. "Remember, we do not practice evil here."

Fern sighed. "Am I expected to join that group?"

"That's up to you. You're not required to, and no one will question if you decide not to."

What a relief!

Fern returned to the village and did her chores. That afternoon when she meditated, Fern explored her feelings about the experience. She found fear, dread, disbelief. Fear of the unknown, of what she didn't understand or want to believe in. She sensed no evil, only a lack of readiness on her part. Taran was right. She had been exposed to so much since she'd been here. Some things she'd embraced, but she resolved to be no part of this girls gathering. The only power she wanted to develop was wrashiru, so she could go home.

After this, the girls who had been involved in the Light Gathering treated her no differently than before. No one spoke of the event.

CHAPTER 22
ERUPTION

The small moon was waxing. Taran reminded Fern, "The anniversary of your birth is approaching."

"Tekuyate."

"Do you feel better now?"

"Oh, yes." The next time she meditated, ethenos was successful. Perhaps it was the pull of her sisters' thoughts about her. She found them in the kitchen helping their grandmother frost a cake. The youngest asked, "Are we going to put candles on it?"

Grandma said, "Why do you want candles?"

"For Fern. It's her birthday."

They remembered!

"But Fern's not with us anymore. She's in heaven."

"No, she's not. She's someplace else. She told us."

With a patronizing smile, their grandmother said, "We can put candles on it if you want to. How many?"

The ten year old said, "Fifteen."

With tears in her eyes, Fern watched them count candles and set them on the cake. She stayed until after supper when Grandma brought out the cake. Her sisters insisted on singing "Happy Birthday" and Grandpa took ice cream out of the freezer.

"I really miss Fern," the little one said.

Grandma wiped away tears. "We all do."

Fern woke in the morning feeling older, more mature. She confided to Tira, "I'm fifteen now. How old are you?"

"Ten Full Moons."

* * *

Digging a new latrine was always dirty work. One day after such an assignment, Fern bathed and washed her tunic in the pool by her mother's hut. She laid it out to dry and went into the hut to meditate. When she returned for her clothes, she was surprised to hear voices upstream. A couple was splashing in the water of an uphill pool, unclothed, of course. Before she could gather her tunic and hide herself, they saw her and waved. Blushing, Fern hurried into the hut to dress and was careful not to look upstream when she returned to the village.

Later, Taran spoke to her. The couple had told him about the encounter. "We've tried to be considerate of your inhibitions," he said. "But when you close your mind so tightly against us, we can't keep track of your whereabouts or your needs. Roni and Torbil are sorry they embarrassed you. They wouldn't have been in that creek had they known you were there. Let us know when you want privacy."

Fern was now doubly embarrassed. "Am I like a baby that I have to be kept track of?"

"In a way, you are. You still don't know all the ways of our world and need to be kept safe."

"I never asked for special treatment."

Her parents would have reacted emotionally to this huffiness and an argument would have ensued. Fern was in the mood for a good blow off, but Taran merely half-smiled, and she knew the discussion was at an end. She returned to her mother's hut to sulk until suppertime.

* * *

When the small moon was full, Fern made another mark on the post in her mother's hut. How many more must she make? Good thing it's a big post, she thought.

Another wave of despairing loneliness settled over her. Insomnia returned. Her pointless longing for Tiril had not dissipated and now she missed him more than ever. She tried to contact him mentally but was unsuccessful. His promise to check on her sisters was some consolation. Despite Andli's nurturance, she missed her mother terribly. Taran was wise and compassionate, but he was not her father. Rina and Doran treated her like a daughter, but she could barely converse with them. Sometimes she could confide in Tira, but she continued to harbor resentment against this would-be sister, and she didn't know why.

On her darkest days, Fern grumbled about the discomforts inevitable to their lifestyle, including sitting on the ground all the time. She resented the mindless chores, especially fetching water and firewood. She didn't see any reason to thank the river for water, but if she filled her vessel without doing so, anyone nearby would react as though stung by a nonexistent insect. No one remarked on her moods, but sometimes she noticed what looked like pity in others' eyes. If she told Taran she didn't feel like a lesson that day, he didn't press her.

Fern no longer went with a group to gather firewood. The solitude of the forest was a balm for her soul, yet she hated the drudgery of hauling wood. It seemed silly to go so far to find dead wood when they were surrounded by trees. She never took living wood, but one day when she didn't feel like walking any further, she noticed a tree with a dead limb. Why wait until it dropped? She grabbed it and pulled. As it fell, her heart seemed to jump inside her and settle into sadness. When she picked up the dead branch, she notice a living vine attached. Not only had she robbed the vine of its support, she'd unwittingly uprooted it.

"Estut miryit." Fern tried to restore its roots to the soil. Then she rebelled. "This is crazy. Plants don't have feelings." She intended to strip the dead branch of its living attachment, but something stopped her. With a sigh, she leaned the limb against the tree, returning the vine as much as possible to its original condition. "I really am sorry," she said to both vine and tree and walked deeper into the forest to fill her sling.

* * *

Not all her days were dark. She helped Andli finish Tala's new tunic. Fern's skills in fabric arts now surpassed those of other family members. Andli let her gather and process the reeds and take more initiative in preparing dyes. Fern could envision the finished product, and weaving was a pleasure. Others in the village occasionally asked for Fern's help, which added to her sense of self-worth.

But when the small moon grew full once more and she made another mark on the post, She was thrown back into hopelessness. She isolated herself again, spending her days in her mother's hut spinning, or in the wilderness gathering food and firewood.

Because she lacked Doran's knowledge of the forest and couldn't find the caches of dead wood he led groups of children to, searching for firewood took Fern on long hikes. The upside was, these daytime rambles showed her new paths to take on sleepless nights. One such night, she noticed a red light in the western sky. It was too late to be the afterglow of sunset, so she set out in that direction. The moons lit her way through the woods.

Beyond the trees on the crest of a ridge, the sky appeared to be on fire. A forest fire? How close? Her heart pounding to the cadence of the distant blaze, she followed the ridge to a cliff overlooking a stony valley. Across that valley, a black mountain rose against the sky. From its peak raged a conflagration. Immense billows of red and black and orange grappled with one another in a frenzied dance. A distant roar echoed across the valley and the wind bore a faint stench.

Fern's heart froze. It was an active volcano!

Did anyone else know about this? How far was it from the village? Was she safe here on this ridge? She must go warn everyone! She turned to run, caught her foot on something, and sprawled onto her face. Too alarmed to feel pain, she managed to collect herself, brush off the dirt, and temper her panic.

She heard no sound, but sensing a presence, looked up. Taran stood beside her. "Do you see that?" She pointed to the volcano.

"Yes," he said. "We've been watching it. There seems to be no danger right now, but we remain vigilant."

Fern felt foolish. Of course he'd know what was going on in the neighborhood. Her leg began to throb. She sat down and rubbed it. It bled a little, but she could walk.

She stood beside Taran and gazed at the burning mountain. She pointed at the valley and said, "That's the lava field we went to with Darsan, where we collected rocks. Tiril said the volcanoes were extinct, or dormant."

"We thought they were," Taran said. "We're not all-knowing." After a few minutes, he asked, "Are you ready to go back?"

She nodded. He led the way, choosing an easier path for their descent. It was nearly daylight when they reached the village.

CHAPTER 23
CALAMITY

On sleepless nights, Fern continued to climb that ridge to check on the eruption. No one else seemed as anxious as she, at first, but as days passed she became aware of a growing restlessness in the village. Andli enlisted her in weaving moccasins of tough cord for every member of the household, then for others in the village. Rina and a few others made more "bamboo" water bottles.

One day, Andli helped Fern attach straps to her basket to make a backpack, then they lined it with waterproof cloth. Everyone's basket was similarly modified.

Fern asked, "What is going on?"

Taran said, "We may have to evacuate."

The parents assembled the children in front of the house. Rina placed a bowl and a few other items in the bottom of Ara's backpack and gave instructions. Taran translated for Fern. "You'll be required to carry this much and some food. Leave room in your basket for your bed clothes and spare tunic, then pack whatever else you wish to take, but remember, not more than you can carry."

Fern swallowed. "If we have to go, will we come back?"

"It all depends."

The red glow became visible from the village at night and sometimes the wind carried the smell of smoke and brimstone. When she climbed the ridge, day or night, Fern found other watchers, usually sitting in meditation. If they didn't speak to her, she didn't bother them.

Her depression gave way to mounting anxiety. She wanted to do something besides make moccasins. One day Simbi ran across the sameg in tears. Fern asked what was wrong. Simbi was too upset to give an intelligible answer, so Fern asked Tira for help.

Tira spoke with Simbi's mother, then told Fern, "Simbi wants to put her doll in her backpack, but Farsa won't let her."

"Why?"

"The doll can be replaced. Simbi is expected to carry her clothes and blanket, but that's all she can take. The doll won't fit."

Fern looked at Farsa, who was by now very pregnant. "She can't carry it for her?"

Tira shook her head. "Farsa isn't expected to carry anything except her baby. Her mate Belan will take her things."

"I'll carry it for her," Fern volunteered. "I don't have much."

Tira related this to Farsa, who almost cried in gratitude.

Fern took Simbi and the doll to her room and put the doll in her backpack. Tira explained what she was doing in Human Talk. Simbi hugged Fern.

The miaven tree on her mother's grave continued to bloom, and the sapling on Nasi's grave also blossomed. One day when she watered the trees, Fern wondered how a volcanic eruption would affect these and the other plants in the surrounding forest. She grieved for them. On a whim, with the tree's permission, Fern picked a few flowers and laid them on the seat of her mother's rocking chair. If there was one thing she wished she could take with her, it would be the chair, but it was too heavy for her to carry any distance, and she knew it would be frivolous to ask anyone else.

One evening when Fern bathed in the creek by the hut, she noticed the water seemed warmer than usual. By morning, it was too hot to touch. She couldn't find Taran or make her meaning clear to anyone else, so she told Tira, who informed Rina. When Rina put her hand in the water, she cried out. Then she stood, looked around, and pointed upstream. Above the trees rose a column of steam. Rina spoke to Tira and hurried back to the village.

"Finish packing your basket," Tira said. "And grab your hat and moccasins."

Fern snatched her spindle from the hut and ran home. She packed thread she'd spun but abandoned her collection of rocks, except for the little egg-shaped one. She slipped that one into the pouch that held the lock of her mother's hair. She thought about Tiril. His mandolin hung in the other room. She hated to leave it but, like her rocks, it could be replaced.

There was plenty of room for Simbi's doll. Fern watched the other girls pack, in case they needed her to carry something. Tala and Ara tucked their dolls beneath their blankets and spare tunics. She noticed a doll lying on Tira's stripped bed. She didn't know Tira had one.

Tira shook her head. "It's okay. I don't need her anymore."

When Fern passed through the main room, she noticed Andli remove several balls of thread from her own backpack and lay them aside with a look of regret. Andli was abandoning some of her prized possessions as well as thread she'd spun and dyed. Fern loaded Andli's balls in her own basket and, before Andli could finish repacking, took some additional thread from Andli's and put it in hers. Andli gave Fern a grateful smile and replaced her jewelry in her backpack.

Soon nearly everyone in the village was assembled on the sameg. Skri wrapped in leaves and flour packed in pouches were distributed. Everyone carried a share. Sela and another young mother carried only their babies on their backs. Fern suspected Rufan and other adults carried their loads for them. The stronger men had larger baskets than anyone else. Each adolescent was put in charge of a young child. Simbi gladly took Fern's hand. Tira was given Ara.

The sky grew overcast, but not from rain. The heat increased, but not from the sun. Doran took the lead and the families followed. Some of the grandparents and elders trailed in the rear. Taran and a handful of the more athletic men and women had their baskets ready but stayed behind. Others, including his grandparents and the weka, appeared unprepared to travel.

"What about them?" Fern almost shouted. "Aren't they going?"

"They'll be okay," Tira replied. "They're not strong enough to carry a load all the way to the sea."

"So we're just going to leave them to die?"

"No. They will find their own way."

No time for conversation. They headed down river. As they rushed through the meadow and past the burial ground, Fern picked one last flower from the miaven tree on her mother's grave and stuck it in her hat. Doran led the group onto a path in the woods that would take them uphill to the east.

Suddenly, there was a rustling in the leaves above them. Dark shapes flew through the branches. Fern stopped and looked up. It couldn't be birds.

"Run!" someone behind her screamed. When a black rock hit the ground beside her, Fern picked up Simbi and ran. A loud boom echoed across the distance. Doran led them behind a fold of the mountain which shielded them from the barrage. Fern set Simbi down and they cowered with the rest of the villagers against base of the cliff while rocks rained down on the forest, shredding trees and breaking limbs. The stones didn't look hot but they sparked fires.

Before Fern's heartbeat slowed, the hail of rocks slackened. She noticed Alta sitting on the ground, as though she were tired. The last rock fell. In the silence, no one moved. Fern looked at Doran, but his attention was on Alta, who appeared to be in deep meditation. Finally, she opened her eyes, stood up, and spoke to Doran.

"Follow us," he said. "Stay in our path."

He and Alta slowly wound their way uphill, avoiding obstacles and fires, the villagers close behind them.

When they came to a place with no fallen stones, they paused to rest. Fern noticed that Taran and the ones who'd stayed behind were still missing. She set down her load and thought of going back to look for them when Taran, Rina, and a few others appeared among the trees, covered with sweat from running. Fern sank to the ground in relief. "You're safe! How?"

Taran took a draught of water from his bamboo before answering. "We took shelter under the waterfall when the mountain exploded."

"Why didn't you come with us?"

"We remained behind to put up a shield so that the rest of you could escape safely. We can't stop an eruption, but we diverted the ash and gases from blowing this way. Those of us who are traveling by foot had to leave. The others are maintaining the shield. When it becomes too dangerous, the ones who can will wrashiru to safety." He drank more water.

"And the others? What about the weka?"

Taran looked directly into her eyes. She could see the pain in his. "Dorsa and Geltan have decided they have lived long enough, and plan to disembody."

She jumped to her feet. "No!"

"That is their choice." His voice was hoarse, but not from exertion. "They are ready and will suffer no pain."

Fern looked at Rina, who was also the couple's descendant. She smiled sadly at Fern and put her arms around her. After a few tears, the distress lifted from Fern's heart.

They trudged on the rest of the morning without stopping. No one sang, channeling their breath and energy into putting more distance between themselves and danger. Simbi got tired and sat down. She got up only when Fern offered to carry her basket for her. Farsa was pale with exhaustion.

They stopped for lunch and much-needed rest on the crest of the ridge. Fern's legs ached almost as much as they had during her first days here. No one took time to gather lenitrus, so they ate only skri. Nearly everyone lay down for a nap. Fern laid her head on her backpack and immediately fell asleep.

She half woke to sounds of a storm. A few elders sat in deep meditation, keeping them dry. The rain cooled the air. Before they left the ridge, Fern looked back in the direction of the village. In the distance she saw a forest fire that no rain could quench. Their village was burning, along with the miaven trees, her mother's hut, and all it held.

Taran spoke softly. "Our village was in the path of a lava flow. Not from the mountain we'd been watching, but from another fissure that opened, uphill from the village. Your diligence in observing the water temperature helped us get out in time." He swallowed. "We will not be going back."

Fern went numb. A homeless, motherless child, again. She gave herself no credit for saving her people. In a small voice she said, "Where will we go?"

"We'll go to our cousins who live by the sea and stay with them until we can find a new home."

"This way," Doran called. Fern felt a soft warmth in her hand and looked down into Simbi's anxious eyes. She gently squeezed the child's hand and forced her body to move forward.

They walked downhill for a while, which proved almost as difficult as climbing, with loads to carry and children to restrain from sliding down too fast. Fern made herself strong for Simbi's sake but was more concerned about Farsa, who stoically kept moving. When they reached the little valley at the bottom of the ridge, they followed a creek downstream and refilled their water bottles before climbing the hill on the other side.

Now that danger was not so imminent, their pace slackened. They rested at the top of the hill. "How much farther until we're safe?" Fern asked Taran.

"We're out of danger now, but we'll go on a little further today."

"How long until we reach the sea village?"

"Several days. We couldn't take our usual path because of the eruption. We have to find another way."

They made camp by the little river in the next valley. Fern took Simbi's doll out of her backpack and handed it to her. "Tekuyate," Simbi said and, hugging the doll, returned to her parents. Ragged moccasins were repaired and dirty tunics and bodies washed in the stream.

The younger people gathered lenitrus, and Alta built a fire. The elders set flat rocks around it and baked pancakes for supper. Rina spread a cloth for pancakes and the family sat in a circle around it. They topped the pancakes with lenitrus and dressing and ate, breaking off pieces of pancake and rolling them around the lenitrus.

There was no dancing that night, only soft, plaintive songs with hopeful, healing refrains. Most of the musical instruments had been abandoned, but Jorsil had his flute. Fern let the melodies flow through her, but she couldn't sing. She had left behind every remnant of her former life. No longer could she visit her mother's grave with its flowering tree or rock in her chair. And the post in her mother's hut where she'd kept track of time—all gone.

As Fern prepared for bed, she found, still tucked in her hat, the miaven flower she'd picked that morning, by now wilted. She put the flower inside the pouch with her mother's lock of hair and the egg-shaped stone.

One of the elders spoke her name. Another repeated it.

Tira nudged her. "Taran called you."

Fern saw Taran sitting by the fire. He stood and faced her as she approached. Everyone else stood as well. Bregan spoke to her but she caught only a few of his words. Then Torbil said something, then Alta.

Taran said, "Fern, we are all grateful to you. We have lost our homes, but we still have our lives. If you had not alerted us to the danger of the second eruption, many of us would have perished. We will always be grateful for what you have done."

In unison, everyone said, "Tekuyate."

"Tekuyate," Fern responded. Then she whispered to Taran, "I really didn't do anything. I just noticed how hot the water was."

He hugged her. "You've done more than you realize." Andli hugged her next, then the rest of the family. By the time everyone else in the village had hugged Fern, she was more than ready for bed.

Using her spare tunic for a pillow, she rolled up in her blanket and cuddled next to Tala and Ara. At long last, she allowed herself to acknowledge the danger they'd faced. A cold tremor echoed down her spine. If she hadn't noticed the hot water, if Rina hadn't spotted the steam uphill from the village... Some of them could wrashiru. Tira could, and Taran, but what about the rest of the family? Andli? She couldn't bear to lose Andli.

How many would have perished? Would she have been among them? She had wrashirued once in an emergency. Could she have done it again? If not—she shuddered. It would be a terrible death. She still carried guilt from failing to rescue her father. If she had been able to wrashiru again, how could she bear the guilt of surviving when others didn't? But—they survived. They were safe.

Relief softened her anguish and gave way to gratitude. Warmth flowed through her. By the campfire, Forsil's flute warbled. Someone sang a lullaby. Fern drifted to sleep.

Sometime in the night, she dreamed of her family on Earth. It was no ordinary dream but had the quality of ethenos. Her little sisters sat at the kitchen table drawing pictures.

"What are you drawing?" Grandma asked.

"Fern. Where she lives now."

"That's nice."

Fern moved closer so she could look at the drawings. Each displayed a figure with yellow hair and a big smile. In one sketch, she wore a red dress and in the other, a blue one. The pictures also showed thatched huts with trees and mountains in the distance.

Fern hugged her little sisters. "You heard me! When I talk to you in your dreams, you can hear me."

* * *

Fern woke in the grey dawn to fragrant, cool air. Mist mingled with the trees. She stretched and nestled against the soft forest floor. Other family members began to stir. She lay still a while, taking stock of her situation. She had lost everything, yet a spark of hope glimmered in her heart.

She couldn't help thinking about the last time she'd escaped disaster, arriving on this world naked, with only her mother. Then she'd lost her, too. Fern stretched out an arm and her hand found her basket. No, she hadn't lost everything. She still had clothing, a blanket for comfort, a few mementoes. More important, she had parents and sisters and brothers. She closed her eyes and listened to those around her folding their blankets, preparing for the day's journey. Love surrounded her. She had all she needed, and more.

"Fern," Tira whispered.

"I know. I'm awake."

A light breakfast consisted of leftovers from supper. Taran, Doran, and a handful of elders stood on the river bank in conversation. The rest of the villagers gathered nearby, watching the east. Fern joined them.

The sun peeked above the mountain, sending its rays through the forest. The villagers sang the morning song. Fern accompanied them in English:

> Light from the stars begins to fade
> And gathers in the sleeping east.
> We bade goodnight to cool, dark hours
> And welcome in the bright, warm day.
> Our hearts are filled with gratitude
> For this green world, blue sky and sea,
> And for the sun and moons and stars,
> And for the miracles of life.

Then Doran faced the throng and spoke, gesturing down river.

Fern asked Taran. "What did he say?"

"We'll follow this river to the sea."

To be continued…

GLOSSARY

Aloa - love
Ahnti – plant with medicinal properties; resembles our resurrection fern
Erguvon – tree with heart-shaped leaves
Esmilu tefi – I love you
Estut miryit – I'm sorry
Ethenos – etheric, or astral, projection
Human Talk – their language
Kirrib - soup
Imbwina – healing vapor given to Fern's mother
Lenitrus – salad greens
Miaven – small, ornamental tree, planted on Fern's mother's grave
Mi manchi – I miss you
Namai – home (Lithuanian for house or home or roof)
Rambit – edible plant with spear-shaped leaves
Salut – hello
Sameg – common area in the middle of the village
Skri – bread
Ta - I
Tekuyate – thank you
Thortles – captors, from whom the people escaped to this planet
Tolit – a plant with milky sap used in dye
Wispis – edible plant with frilly leaves, like our leaf lettuce
Weka – oldest generation living, great-great-grandparents
Wrashiru – transporting (Beam me up, Scotty!)

CAST OF CHARACTERS

Fern's new family:
    Parents: Andli, Taran, Rina, Doran
    Sisters: Tira, Tala, Ara
    Brothers: Jorsil, Donal
  Extended family:
    Rufan, son of Andli and Autin (deceased)
    Sela, his wife, a weaver
    Dorba, their daughter
    Tiril, son of Taran and Lila
    Olan, Andli's brother
  Elders and weka:
    Alta and Hatir, Taran's parents (Alta is the fire maker)
    Noba, Andli's mother
    Bregan, Taran's grandfather, the wood splitter
    Dorsa and Geltan, Taran and Rina's great grandparents
    Nasi, Andli and Doran's great-grandmother
    Torbil, her son
  Ancestors who appear in stories:
    First Parents: Moses and Rila
    Martha, their daughter, the first fire maker
    Tanil, her mate
    Mosa, Hartha, and Rilan, children of Martha and Tanil
    Abraham, their son
    Anli, his wife
    Wosan, Horil, and Rala, children of Abraham and Anli

Hannah, the youngest daughter of Moses and Rila
Others:
    Aldan, young man who gives Fern a belt
    Rondal, little boy who tries to carry too much firewood
    Narvil, young man who gives Fern a necklace
    Darsan, a geologist
    Tirna, his student
    Hansa, a young woman
    Tandil and Gresin, toddlers
    Simbi, a toddler Fern befriends
    Farsa and Belan, her parents

Acknowledgements

I am deeply indebted to the Writers Alliance of Gainesville, which provided inspiration and support for my literary efforts, and especially to members of my writing pod who gave me invaluable criticism and encouragement: Jane Camerlengo, Art Crummer, Jessica Elkins, Richard Gartee, Skipper Hammond, Jena Liggett, Kimberly Mullins, Bonnie Ogle, Stacey Pittman, Joy Southwell, Chantel Rizardi, and Fran Sweeney. And to my beta reader Tristan Bruce, who also designed my logo.

ABOUT THE AUTHOR

Award-winning novelist Marie Q Rogers can be found rambling the back roads, exploring historical sites, or enjoying the mountains. When not traveling, she lives and writes in the woods of North Florida.

Besides *Trials by Fire*, she has authored *Quest for Namai, Season of the Dove*, and *Notebooks Hidden in an Abandoned House*.

Her short pieces have appeared in *Bacopa Literary Review, Pilcrow & Dagger, Eckerd Review*, and *Local Lives in a Global Pandemic: Tales from North Central Florida*. She posts creative nonfiction on her website, marieqrogers.com.

Among her many interests are edible wild plants and herbs. Her knowledge of wild-crafting came in handy in writing *Trials by Fire*.

If you enjoyed this book, please leave a short review on Amazon and Goodreads. Reviews help sell books, and sales motivate an author keep writing.

www.ingramcontent.com/pod-product-compliance
Lightning Source LLC
Chambersburg PA
CBHW022159240626
47153CB00007B/2732